# Praise for Melissa Schroeder's *A Little Harmless Sex*

4.5 Ribbons! "With A LITTLE HARMLESS SEX, Ms. Schroeder gives her readers just that, and so much more. This is a passionate love story that is very satisfying and I give it a very high recommendation."

~ *Laurie, Romance Junkies*

5 Cups! "Ms. Schroeder has written a book that is impossible to put down."

~ *Sherry, Coffee Time Romance*

"Ms. Schroeder writes hot, steamy sex scenes that will have the reader panting for more. Her characters leap from the pages and the plot keeps the reader turning the cyber pages. This reviewer enjoyed this story very much and she would love to have a man like Max herself!"

~ *Valerie, Love, Romances, and More*

"The love scenes are sweet, at the same time that they're hot and sexy. Melissa Schroeder knows what her readers want and definitely delivers it!"

~ *Kerin, Two Lips Reviews*

Recommended Read! Five Angels! "Max is domineering, yet sensitive, and Anna is both giving and yet occasionally aggressive. Their combination is absolutely combustible as shown by the explosive sex, which ensues once they both give into their innermost desires. Melissa Schroeder has done an excellent job creating characters with whom it's easy to sympathize, and just as easy to pull for Max, in his victory of love over fear."

~ *Lynn, Fallen Angel Reviews*

"The love scenes are sweet, at the same time that they're hot and sexy. Melissa Schroeder knows what her readers want and definitely delivers it!"

~ *Kerin, Two Lips Reviews*

"A Little Harmless Sex takes us on a wonderful ride as friends develop into lovers. For Max, he wants all Anna can offer. Both characters are complex and lively. They bring excitement and pleasure to a story that already has an interesting plot. Ms. Schroeder's words flow with ease and will quickly pull you into this story."

~ *Klarissa, Joyfully Reviewed*

# A Little Harmless Sex

*Melissa Schroeder*

A Samhain Publishing, Ltd. publication.

Samhain Publishing, Ltd.
512 Forest Lake Drive
Warner Robins, GA 31093
www.samhainpublishing.com

A Little Harmless Sex

Print ISBN: 1-59998-423-7
Digital ISBN: 1-59998-322-2

Editing by Sasha Knight
Cover by Scott Carpenter



First Samhain Publishing, Ltd. electronic publication: February 2007
First Samhain Publishing, Ltd. print publication: August 2007

# Dedication

To Linda Kusiolek for believing in Max, Anna and me the first time around. You took a newbie author and gave her more help than she deserved. Your faith in my writing has always and still humbles me. But because of your obvious irrational hatred of commas, part of the proceeds of this book is being donated to help you with your therapy to overcome that. It's the least I can do.

Love,

Mel

# Chapter One

"You have to understand, Max, this has nothing to do with you." Cynthia tucked a strand of her blonde hair behind her ear then blinked several times. The sweet smell of jasmine filled the humid Georgia air along with the clink of glasses and silverware against fine china.

Maxwell Chandler stared at his fiancée—strike that—his soon-to-be ex-fiancée, and wondered why she'd dragged him out to lunch just to dump him. It would have been so much easier and cheaper if she had just called or sent a note. Hell, Max would have been happy with an email telling him to fuck off. But then, that wasn't Cynthia's style.

Cynthia probably worried he'd cause a scene. Max never made a scene. It would be bad for business. Which meant that she didn't know him well. And as his best friend Anna had pointed out, that wasn't any way to start a marriage.

She'd claimed that if you were going to marry someone, you should know every single bad habit that person had. That, in her humble opinion, was the only way to tell if you truly loved the person. He probably didn't know much more past Cynthia's surface than she knew past his. Maybe that's why all he felt was...relief.

"You're calling off our engagement, so I think it has a little to do with me," Max said in an agreeable tone. "Have you met someone else?"

Her blue eyes widened and a look of complete horror passed over her face. "No. It's not that."

"So, you're just dumping me because you don't like me?" Max tried to sound a little hurt. Truthfully though, the tension eased out of his shoulders and the constant throbbing in his head lessened. He'd gotten so used to the pain, Max hadn't realized how intense it had become. Showing his true feelings would be in bad form. Sort of like making your fiancé pay for lunch when you planned to dump him.

Cynthia reached across the table and grabbed his hand. A look of acute distress marred her perfect face. Her eyes filled with tears. She spent most of her days with that look on her face. Any tiny thing set the woman off, and not in a pleasant way. Not that she would ever cause a scene. Cynthia Myers never lost her temper, never showed an ounce of passion.

What had he been thinking when he proposed to her? It couldn't have been because the sex was great. It was good, but someone who stressed out when she had to pick the color of her car couldn't relax enough to have fun in bed. He came, but there was no real satisfaction in fucking the woman. She didn't like wet, hot, messy sex. He'd had to invest in lubricant for the first time in his life. Why marry a woman who couldn't get wet?

"No, I like you a lot. It's just that...well, I think we aren't suited." She picked at the linen tablecloth nervously. Her attention was apparently captured by the complexities of the ivory color and the wrinkle she eased away with her index finger. Without looking at him she said, her voice filled with anxious worry, "I hope there will be no hard feelings."

In Max's opinion, what Cynthia hoped was that he wouldn't take this out on her father. Their families had been doing business for years. It was one of the reasons he'd proposed. And probably one of the reasons—if not the main reason—that she'd agreed to begin with. That and her father had wanted the match. Cynthia usually did anything her father wanted her to do. Well, until today. And the fact that Max had been ready to marry her based on a business relationship didn't say much for him. From the very beginning of their "courtship", Cynthia had seemed like a nervous rabbit. Not once had he ever seen her relax, which explained why she didn't like sex and probably never would.

Max smiled and did his best not to look too relieved. "No. You should know me better than that."

Cynthia looked up, worry puckering her brow, but then she returned his smile, albeit warily. "That's nice to know. I think it best if we tell our parents right away. Daddy is going to be furious."

"Tell him it's my fault."

She sniffled a bit, wiped her nose and then the tears disappeared. "You are a true gentleman."

No, he was a true putz, but he knew Cynthia's father. Max felt like a shit because, for the first time, he realized his heart hadn't been with her or the engagement. "Just tell him I had second thoughts. We're months away from even picking out the invitations. No harm done."

The smile that brightened her face did nothing more than exasperate him. "I truly appreciate it. You know how Daddy is, and he so wanted this"—she gestured back and forth between them with her hand—"marriage to take place."

She licked her lips and reached for her iced tea. It was then that Max noticed her hand shook as her fingers wrapped around her glass. Being nervous was one thing. Being frightened was a whole other ball game.

When he spoke, he reminded himself to keep his voice calm. One word the wrong way and she might bolt. Or, God forbid, change her mind back. "Your father will get over it, Cynthia. It isn't like I won't do business with him."

Again, she offered him a guarded look, but said nothing more as she took another sip. He understood her wariness because he knew her father. As he watched her drain her drink, his mind moved onto other things. Business mainly. His thoughts kept wandering to calling one of his distributors, meetings, his parents who were on vacation in Greece, and...Anna.

"*Max.*"

Her irritated voice pulled him out of his thoughts to focus on the matter at hand. Which was dissolving their engagement...and gaining freedom.

"Sorry, Cynthia. My mind sort of wandered."

Her eyes narrowed as she studied his face, a frown tugging down the corners of her mouth. "You do that a lot, Max." The sharp rebuke he heard in her voice was the first show of gumption he'd seen from Cynthia. The moment she said it, her face flushed and she looked down at the table. Knowing her father, who was a bastard in the first order especially when it came to Cynthia, she'd been trained never to say a word in defense of herself to a man.

"You're right, so you're probably damn lucky to escape my evil clutches."

She snorted, then covered her mouth, looking around to see if anyone noticed. It took her a moment to compose herself again.

"I'm sorry, Max. I didn't mean—"

"No," he said with a laugh and a wave of his hand, "don't let it bother you. I would rather we parted as friends, wouldn't you?"

This time, the smile she gave him reached her eyes and her dimples appeared. For a moment, her expression lightened, and he felt a completely unexpected jolt of arousal. He'd forgotten just how attractive she was. Which was sad, considering ten minutes ago he'd been engaged to her. Cynthia deserved better than that. Hell, they both did.

"I'd like that, Max. I'd like that a lot."

"I think the best thing to do is show a united front. If your father gives us any problems, I'll handle it. I promise."

Surviving the gossip would probably kill Cynthia, and the only way to avoid that was sticking together in the ending of their engagement. Truthfully, he couldn't care less about it, but she would be mortified by the whispers. And, in the world of dating, it would make him more of a catch if a woman could gain his attention. In their small Georgia town, dating and marriage was a debutante's favorite blood sport. He would be a trophy to fling in Cynthia's face.

After many reassurances that he would handle everything, and that he harbored no ill will, she left. The moment she was gone, he motioned for the waiter and ordered two fingers of whiskey. Max never drank in the middle of the day, but he felt the need to celebrate. Cold, yes, but theirs had been more a wedding of two companies than of two people.

He took a sip of whiskey, enjoying the burn as it slid down his throat. It'd been a while since he'd enjoyed a drink without the irritation of other people.

As he downed the last drops, he motioned to the waiter for another one and knew Anna would approve.

ꕤ

Anna Dewinter stared at her almost ex-boyfriend and wondered why she'd started sleeping with him to begin with. Most women would jump at the chance, and into his bed. Wavy black hair and brooding blue eyes had many women comparing him to Heathcliff more than once in her presence. He did act the part of a tortured hero—when it suited his purposes. Like now as he stared at her as if his life depended on her attention. Lord knows it probably worked on the college girls he usually dated. Those little girls didn't understand it was his ego—not his life—that depended on the attention.

She'd been attracted to him in the beginning. The sex had been...pretty good. His hands were quick and eager and he had the most amazing mouth, which had worked wonders on her pussy. But, as an artist, Brad tended toward the dramatic. Everything was either a high or a low, nothing in between. Nothing just level. It got old—fast.

Anna sipped her latte, trying to ignore her frustration, and glanced around her restaurant and coffee house, *The Last Drop*. The lunch crowd had dwindled, but several customers lingered.

*Another good month or two...*

If she kept it going, she'd be able to open that second location in Valdosta she was planning. With the college there, a storefront somewhere near the campus would clean up. She could even plan some weekend events, like maybe a few local performers or a poetry slam. The college groupies would pay a fortune for designer coffee and snacks, along with a few extras. She would make a killing.

"Anna, are you paying attention to what I'm saying?"

Brad's voice interrupted the thoughts of expanding her business. Guilt sent a wave of heat to her face and Anna turned her attention back to him. His bottom lip drooped into a pout. Anna sighed. She really liked him, but Brad tended to take things a little too seriously. He was too young to be so serious. Besides, they'd had some fun and now he wanted to complicate things. His eyes spoke of the pain he thought he felt. Which she knew he didn't. Men his age—or about any age—didn't get their feelings involved in a three-week affair.

Anna sighed again. He was *not* going to make this easy on her.

"Listen, Brad, we had a good time, but I thought we weren't going to take each other seriously."

"I took our relationship seriously, Anna. I can't believe you're dumping me." His voice rose and several of the customers sitting close to her table looked in their direction.

"You said you didn't want to get serious. Your art was the only thing that mattered at the moment."

"Until I met you." His voice spoke of his anguish.

She tried not to notice that more people were paying attention to them. An older couple kept glancing their way, the woman looking a little uncomfortable. It wasn't like Anna had the best reputation in town because of her personal life, but it had never boiled over into her business. She'd be damned if it would now.

"You said that last week."

He paused, then leaned forward and pronounced—with much conviction, "I've changed."

No, what Brad meant was he thought he'd be the one to dump her. She had stolen his thunder and if there was one thing Anna understood, it was men's egos and how they could ruin a woman's life. She'd been down that road before and she wasn't ready to take the trip again.

"It's been fun, and we had a good time, but really, Brad, we've run our course."

"Do you care so little for my feelings?" His voice cracked on the last word.

*Oh, God.* He sounded like he was going to cry. Never again. Never again would she tumble into bed with an artist. No matter how talented his hands were, how enthusiastic he was or how much she needed a good fuck, they weren't worth the trouble. A value pack of batteries was a better deal—and a lot less trouble.

"I care, Brad."

And she did. She'd been drawn by his talent and his sense of humor, as well as his looks. And he was a wonderful man. But he didn't want a long-term relationship any more than she did. He was young, and scared to move on. It was her job to give him a little push.

Anna cleared her throat and tried her best to sound soothing and not irritated. "But you said yourself you were thinking of moving up to Athens at the end of the month. I think that will be good for you."

He stood, his frown still deep, unshed tears in his eyes, and spoke rather loudly. "I thought you cared about me, about my art." Then he stormed out of her restaurant and, Anna hoped, out of her life.

"That was intense." Myra sighed dreamily as she refilled Anna's coffee. At eighteen, Myra still thought dramatic scenes were romantic. At twenty-seven, Anna just found them aggravating and time-consuming.

She rose to her feet and allowed the tension to drain out of her as she glanced over at Myra. Short and small-boned, with fair skin, light blue eyes and pale blonde hair, Myra always reminded Anna of a fairy or water sprite.

"Why don't you take your break, Myra? I can handle this crowd for thirty minutes."

Myra looked ready to agree, then something over Anna's shoulder caught her attention.

Anna turned, annoyance boiling in her belly, sure it was Brad returning to give it one last try. When she saw Max striding toward her, all that irritation melted into warmth. Because he was her friend, her *best* friend, and she loved him. Like a friend.

Friends had really hot oral-sex dreams about each other—didn't they?

She smiled. He responded with a grin that sent a wave of heat tingling along her skin. Every hormone in her body did a little jump to stand at attention. She hoped he attributed her hard nipples to the AC as she forced herself not to rub them.

"Max, what are you doing here in the middle of the day?" Anna hugged him. The familiar scent of his aftershave, mixed with whiskey, surrounded her. Something was up, because Max never drank before five.

"Took a long lunch." His absent tone told Anna his mind wasn't really on her or their conversation. "You busy?"

"I was going to let Myra—"

"Don't worry, Anna. I can wait a little bit." Myra eyed Max with her usual guarded admiration.

Myra was wary of Max. Most people were. Over six feet tall and big-boned, Max hardly ever smiled, giving the impression that he was always serious. Which was true in a lot of ways. But he did have a wicked sense of humor, drier than the Arizona desert. With his chocolate-brown eyes and wavy blond hair, Max should have looked like a big teddy bear. Dressed in a slate gray suit, a black shirt and red tie, he appeared lethal. And dangerously sexy. Oh God, was he sexy.

Anna cleared her throat. “Want something to drink?” He shook his head. “Okay. Why don’t we head on back to my office?” She grabbed her coffee and led Max to the small room behind the service counter.

Entering first, she headed for her comfy desk chair. Max closed the door behind him. When she’d taken over the restaurant a couple years ago, the tiny room had been painted gray, with much of it peeling off. She’d painted the room lavender, giving it a softer appearance, and hung a large mirror behind her desk. It helped give the illusion that the room was bigger. If she was going to be stuck handling paperwork, she wanted to make sure she didn’t feel trapped in a square box. She didn’t do well in any kind of box, square or otherwise.

Anna slid her sandals off and propped her feet on the desk, showing off her blue nail polish and the new toe ring she’d picked up in Gainesville. She took a sip of her coffee and set the mug down. “What’s up, Maxwell? You don’t take off in the middle of the day. Ever.”

“Cynthia called off our engagement.”

Of all the things he could say, that was the last thing she expected. For a few seconds, her mind froze trying to compute what he had just told her. Then, her feet landed with a thud on the floor.

“*She* broke it off?” The woman obviously needed some professional help. Cynthia Myers had been lucky to get a man like Max.

Max shoved his hands in his pockets and rocked back on his heels. One side of his full, sensuous mouth quirked and a zing of heat blazed through her. Her nipples tightened against the lace of her bra. Wet heat flooded her sex. Anna crossed her arms over her breasts.

“Yes. She said we didn’t *suit.*”

Anna snorted. "I told you that five months ago."

"No, what you said is two people as uptight as we were would drive each other crazy in a month."

"I also said the sex would suck. And not in a good way."

Max chuckled and she shivered as the sound sank into her, heating her blood. The man was entirely too sexy for her well-being. He was uptight, as she had said, but something lurked beneath the surface that hinted at a darker, more sensual side. A little part of her wanted to tap into that, unleash it, and see just how wicked he could be.

*Not good, Anna.*

She needed to stay away from all thoughts of sex and Max. Especially since so many of those thoughts ended up with just how wonderful he would look naked and just how wonderful it would be to be naked at the same time. She decided to change the subject.

"Well, I guess it was the day for breakups."

His smile faded and his eyes narrowed. Even looking annoyed he sent her hormones bouncing. It was actually something very odd for her. So many times when a man became difficult—which was a given with any man—she cut him loose. Anna didn't have time or energy to deal with it. But with Max, it seemed to set off another whole level of excitement in her body. Definitely weird.

"You and Brett broke up?"

"No, Brad and I broke up. I wish one of these days you would remember my boyfriends' names." She tried to inject reproof in her voice, but it was hard when a touch of breathless arousal threaded it.

"Keep them longer than four weeks, and I might." Humor lightened his eyes and eased his scowl. Knowing he would brood if she didn't get his mind off his broken engagement, she played along.

"I dated Vic for two months."

"Anna, the man was in a coma for three of those weeks. I don't think you can count that."

She frowned and leaned back in her chair again. "Anyway, he just left right before you came in."

"What's the black look for?"

"Brad made a bit of a scene before he left."

"Ah, young Brad was upset you dumped him." He settled in the chair she had situated in front of her desk.

Because she was truly miffed, when she spoke her voice was a bit sharper than usual as she asked, "What do you mean young?"

"He's two years younger than you." Even though he said it jokingly there was something behind it that bothered her.

"Cynthia is the same age as I am, and that makes her four years younger than you."

He shifted in his chair and stretched out his legs. Max grunted and then changed the subject, which meant he knew she was right and he had no argument. "Anyway, Mom and Dad took it pretty well. I don't think Mom liked her very much. Of course, I'm just assuming everything from the tone of her voice."

"How do they like Greece?"

"I guess okay. No complaints. Mom's just glad Dad isn't messing with Chandler Industries."

"Hmmm. Well, I think this calls for a celebration."

"Celebration?" His bewildered tone made her smile.

"Yes. For the first time in a long time, we're both without significant others at the same time."

His eyes widened, and an emotion Anna couldn't define came and went in them. Which was decidedly odd because after so many years of friendship, she could usually tell what Max was thinking.

"I hadn't thought of that." His voice was void of any emotion.

"I say strawberry margaritas and enchiladas at my place tonight." She paused and he grunted. Knowing him the way she did, she took that as his usual "yes" grunt. "I'll be out of here by four, and then stop off at the store. I have to pick up a couple of things. How about six?"

He rose to his feet slowly. "I guess I need to get back to work."

"See ya later, Maxwell."

He nodded and left, shutting the door quietly behind him. The room seemed a bit cooler and lifeless after he left. Anna's mind drifted into forbidden terrain, which was anything that involved Max and her feelings for him. From the moment he kissed her years ago, she hadn't been able to forget it. If she were truthful with herself, she'd always had a crush on him. After that one little kiss, the crush had turned into full-blown lust, but years of friendship had turned those feelings into something deeper, something much scarier than passion or lust.

Shaking free of those thoughts, she hurried out to relieve Myra and send her home for the day. It was approaching three, and there wasn't much to do other than close up. Anna could handle the books. And John, her cook, could handle the kitchen. She'd have enough time to get home and clean before Max arrived.

And, if she kept herself busy, Anna wouldn't have to think about the fact that she had probably just lost her mind. She'd wanted Max for so long, the temptation with both of them free would probably overwhelm her good judgment. What little of it she had.

Tequila and Max. She licked her lips. A delightfully dangerous mix.

# Chapter Two

Max parked his sedan behind Anna's vintage T-bird convertible and stared at her two-story house.

*What the hell am I doing here?*

He knew exactly what he was doing there. Having dinner with his best friend. The girl he'd watched take her first communion and play flute in her first football halftime. He wasn't there to seduce the utterly scrumptious woman she'd grown up to be. Even if the idea felt much more enticing than anything he'd contemplated in a long time. Just the idea of feeling her skin against his was cutting off the blood flow to his brain.

Max closed his eyes, calmed his breathing and ordered his dick to take a rest. This was not right. The thoughts, his reactions. It was almost incestuous. Their families were friends, and they'd grown up as sort of unofficial cousins. He'd always thought of her as the pudgy little girl with long braids and a mouthful of braces.

Until he returned home after graduating college. She'd lost all the baby fat, developed curves that left his mouth dry and his dick hard, and he'd felt dirty. She had been barely eighteen, and all he'd been able to think of was sliding his cock into her round, warm body.

A bead of sweat rolled down his back and he opened his eyes. Sitting in an enclosed car, in the heat of a Georgia summer evening, was probably not a good idea. No better than lusting after a woman he had no right to even think of that way. Disgusted with himself then and now, he got out of his car, grabbed the bottle of wine he'd brought and headed up the front path to her house.

She'd been planting again, he thought as he eyed the dying daisies in the flowerbed. For all her dedication to her business, charities and friends, Anna failed in one thing. Gardening. It was something she just couldn't accept she couldn't do. She always had such good intentions, but never seemed to pick out the right flowers and always forgot to water them. The abandonment cost many an innocent flower their life.

As he neared the front steps, the sound of hard southern rock drifted through her open windows. A light breeze shifted the curtains and brought the sound of her uneven voice to him. He smiled as she strangled one particularly high note.

He knocked on her screen door and she peeked around the corner of her kitchen. Her dark curls, dampened with perspiration, clung to her neck and forehead. Even through the mesh of the screen, Max could see a glow to her skin. In his mind, he knew it was due to the heat of the day and her kitchen. His hormones had different ideas. They were positive she would look just like this after sex. Hot, wet, messy sex. The ball of lust that had gathered in the pit of his stomach curled tighter. Heat singed a path to his cock as he grew harder.

She smiled. "Come on in. Just getting the enchiladas in the oven. I think I'll have to turn on the AC."

He opened the door and stepped into her foyer. As always, the color explosion in her home momentarily stunned him.

Why, he didn't know. Anna surrounded herself with color at all times.

Golds, reds and purples graced every corner of her home. Knickknacks littered the surface of the tables and were outdone only by her many framed photos. Most were pictures of the two of them. The clutter should have driven him crazy since he liked everything in its proper place. But the dizzying array of furniture, art and odd little "discoveries"—as she liked to call them—was completely innate to Anna. Her house would look as if a stranger lived there without it. It just looked right. Probably because he'd always seen Anna as a kaleidoscope of mesmerizing colors.

"Hey, Max, could you shut the windows in the living room?"

"No problem."

Max set the wine he'd brought on the table in the hallway and went through the process of closing the many windows in the living room and dining room. Even though it was small, he liked her house.

A long group of windows added light and a feeling of openness to the living area. The view of the woods behind her house just reinforced the homey feeling. Anna, being who she was, used every bit of space in the house. If there was a corner, she had something in it. Be it a bookcase, table or a beanbag chair, Anna made sure it wasn't wasted.

Max walked into the kitchen to find it empty. The temperature jumped about ten degrees from the stove and oven, and the scent of cumin, peppers and onions filled the air. Here there wasn't much clutter.

Long counters were organized and clean for working. When she'd bought the house, she'd spent a fortune to have the entire kitchen redone. Marble counters, wooden floors and only the best appliances would do. The one kind of plant Anna could seem to keep alive were herbs, which she grew in pots on the windowsill in her kitchen. Anna's steps sounded on the stairs, and he knew she'd run to shut the upstairs windows.

He slipped around the corner to grab his wine and then headed back to the kitchen. Anna walked in as he searched for a corkscrew in her kitchen drawers.

"Forget the wine tonight, Max." She moved toward the stove and fussed with the rice.

Her skirt brushed the top of his shoe. Anna liked full broomstick skirts with lots of color, and spandex T-shirts one size too small. Like the one she was wearing at the moment. The red fabric cupped each breast tightly. Blood rushed to his groin at the sight of her taut nipples beneath the spandex. Her scent, something sweet and infinitely Anna, mixed with the aroma of the hot spices she was working with. Drawing in a deep breath, Max felt his head spin. He knew she would taste like that. Sugar with a bit of bite.

*Lord have mercy.*

Clearing his throat, wishing he could clear his mind of his last thought, he said, "I brought your favorite kind." He turned the bottle so she could read the label.

As she continued to work the rice, she squinted down at the bottle. "We'll have it next time. I told ya we were having margaritas."

Yeah, she had. That's why he brought the wine. Anna always got a little wild when tequila and triple sec were involved. She tended to get a bit free with her hands. Considering his present state of lust, it was probably not a good idea to test it tonight. The thought of Anna out of control was a little too tempting. Tonight, there were no barriers, no fiancées and no young men to keep him on his best behavior.

"So, are you going to tell me about your big breakup with the writer?" He leaned against the counter as she pulled out her blender.

She rolled her eyes. "Artist, Max. And there isn't much to tell. He kept talking about moving to Athens, so I gave him a little push." She set the red KitchenAid blender he'd bought her two Christmases earlier onto the counter next to his hip. "I picked up some strawberries from that little place over in Valdosta where you can pick them right off the plant. Should be wonderful in the margaritas."

Anna opened the refrigerator and bent at the waist looking for the strawberries. The outline of her ass held him momentarily speechless. She had the perfect rear end for a woman. Anna didn't try to starve herself into a size. Her body had no sharp edges, just rounded flesh that a man could enjoy for hours.

*Think, Chandler, think. Get some of the blood back to your brain.*

"Did you tell your folks?"

She retrieved the strawberries and set them on the counter. "Why would I tell them I found great strawberries for the margaritas?" She padded, barefoot as usual, to her pantry and pulled out bottles of liquor.

He tried not to be irritated by her banter, but he knew she was doing it on purpose. And tonight was not the night to fuck with him. "No, I meant about Brett."

"*Brad*, and no I didn't. Why would I?"

He watched her as she put the bottles of liquor on the counter. "You broke up with your boyfriend."

She shot him an exasperated look. "Max, really. Mom and Dad don't take any of the men I date seriously."

He snorted. “Neither do you.”

She opened the bottles of margarita mix and liquor and started to work on her margaritas.

“Don’t start on me. I’m only twenty-seven.” She looked over at him, one corner of her mouth kicking up into a smirk. “I’m not an old man like you.”

“You’re almost twenty-eight. And I’m only four years older than you.”

She sighed and rolled her eyes. It was a normal reaction to him that never failed to irritate him. She thought he was old-fashioned in his thoughts about women. And he wasn’t, except maybe where Anna was concerned.

“You were born old.” Anna began cutting the strawberries and tossing them into the blender. “Whatcha gonna buy me for my birthday?”

Max thought about the Beatles’ LP he’d paid a small fortune for and smiled.

“It’s a secret.”

This he could handle. Camaraderie was normal for the two of them. From the time she’d turned fourteen and they both discovered their wicked sense of humor, they’d always shared jokes with each other. If he could keep her on this track, and his mind off sex, he would be fine. The muscles in his stomach started to relax until she spoke.

“Well, maybe I’ll ply you with liquor and find out all your secrets.” Her sultry southern accent danced over the words and in his blood. Her smile turned seductive and went straight to his dick. Every bit of moisture in his mouth dried up.

*Jesus, I’m in trouble.*

ꕥ

Anna closed her eyes and took another sip of her margarita, enjoying the way the sweetness of the strawberries and sharp tequila mingled together as it slid down her throat. Opening her eyes, she studied Max over the sugared rim of her glass.

The perfectly dressed, down to the straightened tie, CEO wasn't the same man sitting across the table from her. The first thing that struck her was that the tie was missing. She had no idea where it had ended up, but it had disappeared. Instead of the flawlessly combed head of hair, golden strands stuck out as if he'd been rolling around in bed. He brushed his hand through it again and she laughed when the action screwed it up some more.

"Whachew laughing at?"

His sinfully sensuous lips turned down in a frown and his gaze hardened. She never figured Max would look so delicious pouting. Mainly because she'd never seen him pout before. It was something Maxwell Chandler would never do. But it made him so damn tempting. Not that he needed much in that quarter. Breathing apparently was the only requisite he had to have to tempt her.

"Oh, quit trying to be so damn intimidating. It doesn't work on me when I'm sober. Isnot going to work now."

He grunted then bit into a chip and his posture relaxed a bit. As he chewed, his gaze didn't leave her face. The southern rock she'd had playing earlier had long ago faded into one of the Neville Brothers' sultry ballads. The intensity of his eyes sent an alarm off somewhere in her. Before she could get to the bottom of it and avoid the inquisition, he continued.

"I don't understand you."

He sounded delightfully disgruntled. They'd spent more than a few nights hanging out together, but they'd never gotten completely wasted before. Okay, she had, but Max hadn't. Max didn't lose control.

"Why do you want to understand me?" Anna shrugged. "There are times I don't understand myself."

He cocked his head to one side and waited a few seconds to answer as his gaze moved over her. The silence between them stretched, becoming even more evident when Aaron belted out the last few notes of the song. Anna hated it when Max did that, just stared at her as if he were trying to figure her out. He did it all the time and hadn't succeeded in his quest. Restlessness gripped her but she resisted the urge to fidget. She didn't want him to think he'd made her uncomfortable.

"I think you *do* know what you're about."

His authoritative tone worried her. Max tended to fix things—including people. Especially people. That is what she thought his engagement was about from the first announcement. Cynthia was a piece of work and needed all the help she could get. Max probably saw it and thought he needed to fix her. Anna didn't need to be helped in any way. She was perfectly happy the way she was.

Most of the time.

Anna decided to change tactics. "This conversation isn't making any sense."

He shot her one of his lopsided smiles that made her entire soul hum, then picked up his margarita and took a drink. His tongue moved over his lips, licking the last of the red drops from his mouth. All the while she tried to remember she wasn't supposed to yearn to follow his tongue with hers, and then attack his mouth. She could just imagine the way he tasted. Sweet, with a hint of dark desire that called to her. Once the idea formed, it was hard to push it aside, especially considering her alcohol consumption. But she was saved from embarrassment when Max's voice interrupted her.

"You think I don't know why you date these younger men?"

Anna didn't like the tenor of his voice—or the fact that he'd interrupted her musings—so her voice was a bit sharper when she said, "Because they take instruction so well in the bedroom?"

He set his margarita glass down with a click and his eyes narrowed. "You know you alwaysh do that."

"Have sex with young men—as you call them?"

He shook his head. "No. You always try and change the subject when I try and dig."

Maybe it was the multiple margaritas, but she was confused. The course he was taking made no sense to her. Which was odd because most of the time she could follow his thoughts easily.

"Max, honey, I think you need to take a break from the margaritas."

Leaning back in his chair, he crossed his arms over his chest. "Oh, no you don't. Don't try to make this about my drinking tonight." She opened her mouth to ask him what he was talking about, but he forestalled her by saying, "You always change the subject when I get serious. There has to be a reason you have these shallow relationships."

She frowned. "Why would you assume they're shallow?"

"Are you going to tell me that you have deep, meaningful relationships with men you keep around less than a month?"

"Have you been watching Dr. Phil again?" She shook her head in exaggerated pity and tsked. "I told you not to watch that show."

He ignored her sarcasm and plowed on. “I know you, better than your own parents, I bet. There’s a reason you don’t get too serious.”

Because she didn’t like the direction of this conversation, she decided to offer it another path to go down. “Really? Apparently you have the same problem.”

That brought him up short. “I have no idea what you’re talking about. I happen to be engaged.”

She held up her finger to wave it back and forth. “Na ah ah. You used to be engaged. As in formerly engaged. As in single and dateless.”

“Well, I *was* engaged. And I didn’t call it off. She did.”

She snorted. “So, Cynthia finally found one nerve in her body and started thinking for herself.” She took another sip, watching him over the rim again. “You’re not much better than I am, Max. Admit it, you didn’t want to get married.”

“I did. I wouldn’t have proposed to Cynthia if I hadn’t wanted to.”

A sharp jab of pain punched her right in the gut. “Really. Then why aren’t you depressed?”

He paused to take a drink, then said, “I guess I should be. But it just wasn’t...”

As he trailed off she knew she’d won her argument.

“You didn’t love her, did you?”

She ignored the way her heart gave a little leap at the irritated look on his face. The fact that he didn’t love Cynthia shouldn’t have warmed her so much. But it did—and all the way to her toes. She figured getting up and doing a booty dance was bad form.

“So, you’re single and—a fact I have pointed out quite a bit—you’re older than I am.”

"But it doesn't matter as much for me as it does for you."

She narrowed her eyes as she studied him. Knowing what he was going to say, she led him into the corner. "And why does it mean more if I'm not married than it does for you?"

"Well"—he smiled at her—"you're a woman."

"Maxwell Thurston Chandler, your mother would smack you silly for that comment."

He grunted and lifted his chin slightly, giving the appearance of a very dignified drunk. "If you're going to bring my mother into this, I refuse to argue with you." He drained his glass. "Do you have any more margaritas?"

Anna smiled and reached across the table to pat his hand. "Sure thing, Max. A man who knows how to admit defeat is a man who deserves a drink."

Snorting, he handed her his glass. "I'm a man who knows if I said any more you would tell my mother and I'm a man who knows better than to upset his mama."

ꕥ

Two hours later, they'd moved from margaritas to straight shots of tequila. Max wasn't sure how it happened, but Anna had taken control of the evening. She had a habit of grabbing hold of a situation by the ears and pulling it in her direction. It was something they had in common and probably why they made such good friends. The evening had been just what he needed. And, as usual, Anna had known. She seemed to sense what he needed before he knew he needed it. His stomach was full of her enchiladas and Spanish rice, and his head spun from tequila and Anna.

"You know, I think I know what my problem is with men."

Max turned his head, which rested on the back of the sofa, and looked at her. She was sitting closer than he thought so he drew back so he could focus on her upturned face. They had both propped their feet on the coffee table, his big size twelves next to her tiny size fives.

"How small are you?" he asked.

Anna giggled. The joyous sound made him smile as his gaze moved up her body to rest on her face. Damn, but she was gorgeous. She was everything he wasn't. Open, demonstrative, always smiling. As Anna had said many times before, Max concentrated too much on succeeding—on finishing first. Where Max always had a plan, Anna rarely did, and enjoyed herself three times as much as he did.

"Max, I think you've had too much to drink."

Her eyes sparkled with humor. She had the greenest eyes he'd ever seen. No hint of another color, just green. Like the lawn behind his home in springtime. No matter how flamboyant her personality, or how seductive she was, there was always a hint of intelligence in her eyes. Anna licked her lower lip. He followed the movement, entranced by the sight of her tongue flitting out over her fuller bottom lip. His dick hardened as he thought of her using that mouth and tongue on him. His balls twitched as he imagined the feel of her lips moving over his flesh, the heat of her mouth against his cock.

"What I was talking about is my problem with men."

"You don't have problems with men." In Max's opinion, men came too easily for her. For a girl who'd barely dated in high school, she'd made up for lost time. "You date too much."

Anna collapsed against the arm of the sofa in a fit of laughter. "What you mean is I fuck too many guys. I don't sleep with all of them, Max. But, on the other hand, I'm not embarrassed by my sexuality."

"Of course not. You brag about it."

She nudged him with her foot. "I do not. I just don't hide it. And truth is, there's a double standard. No one in this freaking town thinks anything of a man having a sex life, but they still hold the antiquated idea that women are supposed to be virgins or hate sex."

He really wished she would quit talking about sex. Talking about sex was the next thing to having it. Sitting so close, he could feel the heat of her body. It was wreaking havoc with his thought process. She kept talking about sex and each time she said the word it reminded him he couldn't touch. Which just sucked, and—to quote Anna herself—not in a good way.

She poured herself another shot. Lick, drink, suck. Max shifted, trying to ease the ache in his balls. She purred, her enjoyment of the drink almost making him come in his pants.

Anna leaned back against the multitude of pillows piled on her red sofa. Her dark curls spilled over the vibrant colors. She made the perfect picture of a sensual gypsy. His heart smacked against his chest at the sight of her crooked smile.

"No, I think I figured out that I measure every man against you."

The thought of Anna measuring men's dicks with a ruler popped into his tequila-soaked brain. "You measure them? And how do you know how big I am?"

She stared at him for a moment. Confusion clouded her eyes, then dissolved into amusement. Her laughter filled the room.

"No, I don't mean like that. Although you do have very large hands." She took a shot and then shook her head. "No, I meant by the way they act."

"Oh." The heat of embarrassment crept up his neck and into his face. Anna had been right. He'd had too damn much to drink, especially if he was thinking about Anna measuring his dick.

"All I know about you in that regard is the way you kiss. And you're very good." Anna shrugged one shoulder. "I guess everyone thinks first kisses are special, though."

The memory he'd shoved to the back of his brain pushed forward. He'd been home after graduation, full of himself for doing it with honors. He'd come upon Anna crying over some boy. When Anna had told him she'd never even been kissed and begged him to, Max lost control and gave in to the urge that had haunted him for six months, since the last time he'd seen her. He'd dreamed of that kiss, and more, every night for weeks.

Even after returning to work on his MBA, he'd been haunted by the taste of her lips, the feel of her skin and the thought of what it would have been like to sink into her heated pussy. He wanted nothing more than to possess the right to touch her and make her moan. The need to touch her had clawed inside him. It was wrong then, and wrong now. He still couldn't stop the primal animal who wanted her, especially when the sane businessman was shitfaced.

"You know, that probably was a mistake," she said, drawing him out of his memories.

He shook his head, trying his best to clear the newest image he'd invented. "Mistake?"

"Yeah, you're a really good kisser. And then I had to go out with Tommy Reynolds later that month. He couldn't kiss worth a damn. All spit and tongue. You're a tough act to follow."

The laughter faded from her eyes, replaced by something much darker. Desire so potent he felt the singe of it all the way to the soles of his feet. Blood rushed to his groin. Anna leaned closer, her wildflower scent surrounding him, arousing him. She placed her hand on the back of the couch, then lifted her leg over him and straddled his lap. Her skirt flowed over his pants. When she settled on him, the wet heat of her sex warmed his shaft. Max groaned, his body tightening in response. Her hair slid off her shoulders and brushed his chest, tickling his neck.

His lips were within inches of hers. The only thought that came to mind was taste. A stolen peach on a balmy summer morning. Sweet, delicious, irresistible. He desperately wanted to take a huge bite. She leaned closer, tempting him and driving him insane. Her tongue darted out over her plump, full lower lip. When she spoke, arousal deepened her voice. Her sweet southern accent curled around him and into his heart.

"So, Max, since you're so good at kissing, I was wondering how good you are at fucking."

# Chapter Three

Anna's blood heated as it flowed through her like a raging river. How else could she account for the fact that she felt hot from the inside out? It had to be the fever Max caused. Otherwise, she was coming down with the mother of all bugs. She leaned her chest closer to Max, enjoying the heat of him warming her breasts. Every cell in her body throbbed with anticipation as she breathed in the familiar scent of his aftershave. Damn, she wanted to lick him up one side and down the other. Then start all over again, pausing at his most interesting spots.

"Anna." Lust and reprimand intermingled in his voice. For some reason, it really turned her on. Made her feel...naughty. And Anna loved feeling naughty. It was one of her very favorite feelings.

"Max, really. What have we got to lose? We're both unattached."

"I think of you as a little sister." His voice was as hard as his eyes, his hands fisted so tightly his knuckles were white.

For a half a second, Anna's brazen attitude fizzled as heated embarrassment held her immobile. What if she had been reading all the signs wrong? She'd been known to jump to conclusions before, and wouldn't this just be a kick in the ass. She had been drinking quite a bit of tequila. Could she have fooled her mind into thinking he wanted her because she wanted him so badly? From the moment he'd arrived that evening, Anna had wanted to strip him naked and use his body as her own personal playground. No. That wasn't right. She'd wanted him since that first kiss years ago.

Before Anna could allow her doubts to talk her down, Max shifted his weight and his hardened shaft brushed against her clit. They both sucked in a quick breath at the contact. Every other thought scattered at the brief contact except for one—Max wanted her. Anna longed to shout with triumph, but instead she pressed closer, brushing her aching breasts against his chest. Heat vibrated through her, curling low in her belly.

"Now, I've known you for most of my life." She gyrated her hips, pressing harder against his cock. The movement triggered another wave of heat as the length of him rubbed against her clitoris again. "And I really doubt you'd get a hard-on if you thought of me as a sibling. At least I hope not."

His eyes closed and his nostrils flared as he drew in a deep breath. He released a sigh filled with aggravation. "I'm not supposed to feel this way." There was just enough petulant boy and confused man in his tone to make her smile. Poor Max.

"Really?" She rocked her hips and he growled. "What way is that?"

His body vibrated with desire so strong Anna could feel it to the tips of her nipples. Her head buzzed with a mixture of liquor and anticipation. Anna wasn't an inhibited person, but Max had been the exception.

*Until tonight.*

Until she drank too much and gathered her courage. The yearning that had started almost ten years ago when he kissed her bubbled up and this time she couldn't—wouldn't—stop it. Fantasy became reality. She'd dreamed of this moment for so many years, she couldn't believe she finally was given what she wanted most.

Max, at her mercy.

Max opened his eyes. The color of melted milk chocolate combined with that deceptive sleepy look always made her lose coherent thought. Especially when he focused his attention on her. He had a way of looking at her that made her think they were the only two people on Earth. All the lust darkening his gaze sent a shiver of electric current racing along her nerve endings. The heat warming her tummy slid between her legs. Moisture flooded her sex. The pressure grew stronger, sending delightful little waves of arousal threading through her body. He unclenched his fingers and grabbed her hips. Instead of pushing her away as she was sure he intended, his fingers tightened and he pressed her closer.

Anna threw her head back as he slowly moved her over his cock. The ache in her breasts intensified as she arched her back. Max bent his head and nuzzled her breasts, his breath warming the skin beneath her shirt.

He slid his hands from her hips. One reached up to tangle in her hair, the other braced her back. A second later, warm blood shot to molten lava as his tongue circled her distended nipple through the fabric of her shirt. She shivered as his tongue moved over the tip.

"Max."

Max looked up, but didn't stop what he was doing. He held her gaze as his mouth closed over her nipple. Anna couldn't look away. His eyes were hot with desire, hot for her. Never had she seen such undisguised passion in a man's eyes. Something lurked in the shadows of that passion, something more than what she bargained for. Something she made damn sure to avoid at all costs. From out of nowhere, panic rose and swirled in her chest. No one had ever looked at her that way. This was not lust. This wasn't *just* sex.

"Max." Even Anna recognized the fear in her voice, but she didn't care. She didn't like her feelings this exposed. They tended to get damaged in the long run. She willed herself to close her eyes and not look, but she couldn't. It was as if he had some kind of hold over her.

He didn't say a word, but moved from one breast to the other, giving it the same treatment as the first. The wet fabric clung to her turgid nipple. Another wave of desire flashed through her and just like that, the panic dissolved into heated passion. She closed her eyes and moaned his name. Nothing in her life had ever felt so good, so right. His hands slid down her back and cupped her ass. Max pulled her closer, grinding his erection against her.

Oh God, every loving inch of his shaft throbbed against her sex. Jesus, she wanted—no needed—him naked. The urge to grab hold of his shirt and rip it from his body was so strong, she had to curl her fingers into her palms to resist it. The next instant, he stood, keeping her tightly clasped to his body. He placed her on the couch and stretched out on top of her. His body, hard from the physical activities he loved, pressed against her.

Anna looked at him through her lowered lashes and her breath caught in her throat. The dim candlelight accentuated the harsh bone structure of his face. Not handsome in some respects, but blatantly male. And aroused. The dark flush on his cheeks and his hot, chocolate eyes spoke of his need for her.

*For her.*

Max gently brushed away a few of her rebellious curls. "Tell me now. Tell me you don't want to go through with this." His normally rough voice had deepened and seemed to rub along her dampened flesh. “You and I both know this isn’t a good idea. But, God help me, I don’t think I can stop. So, for once in your life, you need to be the one to behave. If you don’t want this, tell me now.”

His words stirred a warmth in her chest, her heart beating against her breast with...lust? No. No, that was too little a word for the feeling vibrating through her now. It almost overwhelmed her with good judgment. She squashed it, pushed it away. She couldn’t deal with that and six feet of hard male on top of her.

“You should know better than that. I can’t be the one who behaves, ever. I’ve wanted you since that first kiss, although I’m sure I didn’t know what it was I wanted. But I want you, now, here. If I don’t touch your skin in the next minute, I think I’ll die.”

Max groaned, the sound full of irritation and acceptance. Another surge of heat sped through her blood. Anna pushed her aching pussy against his hardened cock. Her pulse accelerated as she allowed her eyes to close in surrender.

His hands went to the bottom of her shirt. As he curled his fingers beneath the fabric, the tips brushed against her skin. In one quick move, he yanked off the shirt. Cool air flowed over her heated skin and she shivered. Max took a shuddering breath, and she opened her eyes. His gaze was fixated on her bare breasts. Anna hadn’t worn a bra that evening. The warmth tripled in his eyes and her nipples tingled in response. She’d been the object of desire for men before, but this was Max. The one man she compared all her lovers to, and found them lacking. Hot cream flooded her sex, wetting her for his entry.

Anna watched the multitude of expressions flickering over his face, confusion and regret the two that seemed to dominate. She worried his hesitation meant he was having second thoughts. Then, Max lifted himself off her. He'd come to his senses, or at least sobered up a bit and knew she wasn't someone he wanted to mess with. Disappointment welled up and almost choked her. Blinking to hold back the tears she knew would spill, Anna looked away to avoid the embarrassment of being rejected. She wouldn't allow him to be the one to call it off though. She wanted to spare herself the pain of being cast off—again.

She swallowed the lump of disappointment that clawed at her throat. "Listen, it's okay—"

The sound of his zipper sliding down stopped her. She whipped her head around in time to watch him drop his wallet on her coffee table. It landed next to one of her grandmother's candlesticks, the vibration tipping it over. It crashed almost unnoticed by either of them. Her gaze traveled off his body to his face. Determination shone in his eyes as his jaw flexed.

"There's no backing out now. There is no way you're going to tell me you don't want this. I could feel your wet heat through my pants. You want me, baby. Hell, I can smell your arousal." Desire had hardened his voice, adding a dangerous edge to it. Just hearing it made her shiver.

Another flood of juice filled her sex as he released his cock from his pants. Max was bigger than average, just as she had predicted. His penis jutted out from a nest of curling dark blond hair. He stroked himself, from the base up to the engorged head. Anna wanted to put her mouth there. Wanted to suck him dry and have him come in her mouth. The image that thought produced had her pushing herself up on her elbows, but he gently stayed her with his other hand as he continued to stroke his cock. Anna licked her lips.

"Don't even think about it. I'm about to come as it is. If you suck me, I'll lose all control."

She pushed her bottom lip out into a pout, more than a little disappointed at being thwarted. "But losing control is fun, Max."

Max smiled and shook his head, but said nothing. He pulled several condoms out of his wallet, ripping one off and dropping the rest on the coffee table. After opening the wrapper, he took out the condom and rolled it down the impressive length of his cock. Every bit of moisture in her mouth evaporated. The next moment, he tugged up her skirt, and his nostrils flared at the sight of her bare pussy, drenched in her juices.

A bark of laughter filled the silence. "I should have known you'd be shaved."

He reached down, sliding his finger against her slit. Lifting his hand, he sucked on his index finger. "Damn, that's good."

She'd never seen anything so basic, so primal, in her life, not during sex at least. Fun, raunchy, that she'd had before. The primitive action sent a few alarms ringing but there was nothing she could do. Even if she wanted to deny the possessiveness she saw in his eyes, she couldn't. For Max, sex wasn't a game as it had been with every other lover she'd had. For him, Anna knew that conquering her in every way possible was just as important. Another look she couldn't comprehend passed over his face as he continued to watch her. Before she had time to sort out all the conflicting emotions, he was on top of her, his cock hot and vibrating against her sex.

"Oh, Jesus."

He kissed her neck, her breast, his tongue gliding over the tip of her nipple, then moving to her lips. She opened for him and his tongue slipped inside, moving in and out of her mouth as he slid his dick against her pussy. With each upstroke, he rubbed the head of his cock against her clit.

While Max continued his assault on her mouth, he pinched first one nipple, then the other. The delicious pain heightened her arousal. Not able to hold back, Anna closed her eyes and sobbed his name. Sex had always been good for her, but never in her life had this level of anticipation coursed through her, pushing her to do something she hadn't done in years. Beg.

"Please, Max, now. I need your cock inside me."

Her voice was hoarse with desire. Every nerve ending in her sex pulsed with need. If she didn't have him now, she'd have to hurt him physically.

She didn't have to wait. He guided his cock into her slick channel. Her inner muscles clasped him tight as he pushed further, groaning the whole way.

"Oh God, baby, you're so tight and wet for me." He lifted her legs over his shoulders, tightening her hold on his cock. He slowly pulled out, then slid back in, to the hilt. Finally, every inch of him was inside of her. But it wasn't enough. She wanted to be fucked hard and fast. But Max had put her in a position where he retained control, where he picked the rhythm. Frustration boiled even as he pulled almost all the way out and then thrust back into her.

She wiggled as much as she could against him. "Harder."

He chuckled and pulled out again. This time his thrust back in was rougher, but still controlled. As she watched him, his lips curled in pure masculine satisfaction and dominance.

"I'm going to fuck you like you need to be fucked. No quick screw. I want to push you. I want to make sure you can't control yourself. I want you screaming my name when you come." As he spoke he continued his same lazy rhythm.

Irritation had her lifting herself to her elbows, but Max pushed her down. His hands stayed on her shoulders, pressing her into the couch.

"You asked to be fucked, and you're getting exactly that. You are going to take my dick the way I want you to." His demanding tone should have scared her, or at least angered her. But another wave of juice filled her pussy, wetting his dick further. Never in her life had she been this turned-on.

"Touch your breasts." Without a thought, she reacted to the command immediately. Anna circled her nipples with her fingers. "Now, pinch them." She did. "You like that, don't you?"

Anna nodded as she pinched them again, sending another rush of electricity through her. His measured thrusts were increasing in speed. With each move into her, he pushed her just a little closer to the pinnacle.

"I want to see you come. I want to feel your pussy clenching my dick as you scream my name." His harsh words sent her rushing over the edge into a free fall. "That's it, baby. Yeah, that's it."

"Max!" He thrust harder and faster. The coil drew tighter, then burst into a thousand pieces as her orgasm ripped through her.

"Ahh, Anna." He thrust hard, once more. He exploded as he shouted her name again. She looked up at him at that moment, his eyes closed, a look of sheer pleasure sweeping over his face. He shuddered twice then opened his eyes. The warmth in his gaze was what she expected. But around the edges of it, past the sexual satisfaction, there was something more.

Emotions she hadn't felt, hadn't allowed herself to feel for years, filled her. Tears gathered in her eyes as Anna closed them. The emptiness she'd denied dissolved and was replaced by something deeper, scarier. Panic rose and she pushed the feelings to the back of her heart, her soul. Thinking in terms of love and commitment when her body was still warm from Max was impossible. Because it would ruin the mood, and there wasn't a damn thing she could do to change it.

Max gently released her legs from his shoulders, but Anna wouldn't, couldn't, open her eyes. She didn't want him to know he had brought her to tears. And, truth be known, Anna didn't want to see the regret he would start to feel any moment now. Max settled on top of her. His dick, still pulsing from his release, rested inside of her.

His hands burrowed beneath her ass, a hand cupping each cheek. He sighed, the sound filled with so much sated satisfaction that her heart turned over.

Anna wrapped her arms around him, knowing deep in her soul they may have really screwed up their friendship. There was no way back from this, no way to be just friends. They'd gone over the edge, and turning around and pretending it didn't happen would be impossible. The regret she expected was there, as was the sadness knowing that one day he'd realize they wouldn't work. She knew she was in for a world of hurt.

But in her heart, Anna knew she'd do it again, given the chance.

# Chapter Four

Every muscle in Max's body relaxed, his cock still inside of Anna, as he shifted to the side to give her some relief from his weight. Warmth filled his chest as she followed him and snuggled closer. Anna had never had a problem with showing affection toward him, but he hadn't been quite sure how she'd react after their lovemaking. With all of her boys, she seemed to keep them at a distance. There was sex, always, he thought with a frown, but there never seemed to be any sort of genuine fondness, at least on her part. He knew it was her way of keeping it on a certain level, all about sex. Well, he wasn't going to let her do that. He'd make sure she knew it was more than that. Max drew a deep breath. The musky scent of sex hung in the air. He waited for regret to fill him, but the only thing coursing through his veins was bone-deep satisfaction.

Max pulled Anna even closer, one hand still resting on her rounded ass. Using his other hand, he pushed back some of her hair, his fingers threading through her wild curls. Even though she kept her eyes closed, a smile curved her lips.

*In satisfaction?*

He was sure of it. He kissed her temple. Hot and moist from their lovemaking, her skin smelled of passion and of Anna.

Max closed his eyes as the memories flashed in front of them. The taste of her skin, of her mouth, the way she moaned his name. Nothing had felt as good as sinking into Anna's hot sex. When she had tightened around him...

His dick hardened. He pushed deeper into her. Anna hummed, arching her back. He slid back out and pushed in again, and both of them almost toppled onto the floor.

Anna laughed, and the sound of it skittered across his skin and sank into his heart. "I think we need to head into my bedroom." Her husky voice skated along his senses.

"I agree." Max nipped at her earlobe. "Although, I'll never be able to sit on this couch again without thinking about sliding into you and hearing you moan my name."

Anna shivered and his cock immediately responded. Reluctantly, Max moved away from her, but couldn't resist kissing the tip of her upturned nose. Sitting up, he maneuvered over her. Drawing in a deep breath, he pulled off the condom and threw it in a nearby waste bucket. Max scooped up the rest of his condoms and turned back to face her again. Grabbing her hand, he yanked her to her feet and lifted her in his arms.

"Max!" Exasperation and embarrassment colored her voice.

"What?" He liked the way she felt as he carried her. She was warm and soft. Just like she felt when he slid into her.

"I'm too heavy for you to carry."

He quirked an eyebrow and smiled at her. "I think I've proven you wrong there, Anna. You weigh next to nothing. Besides, doesn't every woman want to be carried up the stairs like Scarlett? Hell, we live in Georgia. It's a rule."

Anna chuckled as she wrapped her arms around his neck. Her fingers played with his hair. The touch had his dick twitching. After undoing a few shirt buttons, she ducked her head and, a moment later, her tongue slid across his nipple. Max almost dropped her when he felt the scrape of teeth over the tip. He took the stairs two at a time and headed to her bedroom. He paused at the doorway.

Since she'd bought the house three years ago, Max had only been in her bedroom once, before she moved in. Before she bought her bed.

The massive king-sized bed dominated the bedroom. He'd actually gone with her when she bought it. It had been a test of wills for him. She'd jumped on the bed, smiling up at him, her dark curls bouncing as she checked out the mattress. The image of joining her on that bed, bringing a smile to her face like that, almost made him pass out at the time. It took every bit of self-control for him not to jump on that bed, in the middle of the store on a Saturday, and strip her naked. Because of that, he knew never to enter her bedroom. If he had, he wouldn't have let her out of the bed until she could barely walk.

The barriers were gone now. Thanks to two broken relationships and a lot of tequila, Max could throw her on that bed and do what he'd been dreaming about for years. Determinedly, he stepped across the threshold and did just that.

Surprise and pleasure filled her gasp. Anna landed in the center of the purple comforter. Her legs were spread and Max caught a glimpse of her bare pussy. Her pink, pouty lips still glistened with her arousal. Another surge of lust pounded through his veins. His balls tightened as Anna rested back on her elbows against the multiple pillows, raising her legs and parting them further for a better view.

*Jesus.*

Max stepped forward and practically tripped over his own feet. She laughed. Anna had a husky laugh that sank into his bones every time he heard it. With her naked it made him almost insane. Max shuddered. Primitive urgings raced through him, heating his blood to boiling. He wanted—no needed—to make her his. He pulled off his clothes, throwing them on the floor behind him. She still wore her skirt so he grabbed the waistband and yanked it off her. He joined her on the bed, serious in his expression, in his actions.

Max settled atop her, the warmth of her sex heating his cock. He closed his eyes and slid his shaft along her slick folds.

Anna hummed. The sound vibrated through her to him. He lifted his upper body, resting his weight on his elbows.

The sight of her simple little smile shot right into his chest. Her rebellious curls flowed around her, contrasting with the pale pink pillowcase. The scent of aroused woman surrounded him.

“You feel good, Max. Very, very good.”

She moved her hips in rhythm with him, humming all the while. Warmth curled in his stomach, crept up into his chest and coiled right into his heart. Before Max could come to terms with what that meant, with what would come to pass from their actions, Anna slipped her legs around his waist.

“Maxwell, hon.” A mixture of sexual longing and frustration colored her voice. Irritated amusement filled him. The woman was trying to control everything. Again.

Before she could assume command of the pace of their lovemaking, he broke free of her legs. Kneeling on the bed, Max looked down at her. The little frown marring her face almost made him laugh. His Anna was a demanding wench. Anna was used to getting her way. She liked controlling those little boys she dated.

“Max, what the—”

Before she had a chance to complain, Max captured her hips and flipped her over to her stomach. She let out a screech, muffled by the pillows.

Anna tried to boost herself up, but he rested his hand in the center of her back. He grabbed pillows with his other hand.

"Get up on your knees," he ordered, his voice rough with need. She hesitated, for just a second, and it aggravated him. But she soon obliged him, lifting herself to her knees. He shoved the pillow beneath her pelvis. Max settled on top of her, sliding his penis between the cheeks of her ass. Her hair tickled his chest.

"Now," he whispered in her ear, "for once you are going to let someone else handle things."

Anna shivered. Not from cold, he was sure, but from desire. His balls tightened in anticipation.

He moved away from her. Again, she brought her hands to the mattress to lift herself, but Max smacked her ass. His hand stung from the slap. Before he could apologize, she chuckled.

She turned her head, pushed her heavy hair aside and looked back at him. Devilment sparkled in her eyes. "Maxwell, I had no idea you were naughty." Her voice was soft and husky and perfect for the bedroom.

"There are a lot of things you don't know about me."

Like how badly he craved this. Being here, being the one to make her scream.

Max skimmed the backs of his fingers down her spine and stopped at the small of her back. Earlier, he hadn't had a chance to see her completely naked, but now that he did, the rose-and-vine tattoo above her rounded ass held him mesmerized.

He traced the intricate design with the tips of his fingers. She shivered again.

"When did you get this?"

"Last fall. You know, when I went with my cousins to Hawaii. We all said we'd get them. I was the only one who did."

Of course Anna did. She always rose to the occasion. She did anything guaranteed to raise a few eyebrows in their little town. It might be the twenty-first century, but Park City, Georgia, tended to be just a bit more conservative than the rest of the country. Anna's independent streak had set her apart from most of the women in town.

Her attitude made her the complete opposite of the women he dated. They usually deferred to him on decisions on every level. From where to dine for the evening to where to vacation. Not one of them made decisions where he was involved.

He'd never realized until this moment how much that irritated him. Of course, none of them got under his skin like Anna. Knowing his self-control was being tested, he grabbed a condom and rolled it on before they went too far. He slid his fingers across her rounded ass cheeks. She wiggled.

"Hmmm, that feels good, Maxwell," she purred.

His erection throbbed. He had to taste her or he would go insane. "Really? Well, if you think that feels good..."

Max took hold of Anna by the hips and flipped her over. She landed with a bounce and a squeak. He covered her body with his and sighed as he reveled in all her soft curves against him. He pressed the head of his dick against her clit. Her warm juices poured over it.

Before she could do anything more than moan, Max kissed a path to her breasts. As he swirled his tongue around one nipple, he teased and pinched the other.

He moved from one turgid peak to the other. He raised his head. Her protest ended with a moan as he blew softly against her glistening nipple, then nipped at the tip, scraping his teeth over it.

Max continued his journey down her body, licking, kissing. When he reached her bellybutton, he stopped. There, glinting in the center, was a belly ring shaped like a zipper.

A surge of heat swept through him and he shuddered. Max had always had a secret thing for belly rings. There was something so sensual, so wicked about them, it sent his blood straight to his cock.

Anna moved restlessly against him and rose, settling back on her elbows. She opened her mouth to protest, but Max slid down between her legs and pressed a kiss at the soft skin of her inner thigh. She didn't say anything, just watched him as he kissed his way to his final destination.

He closed his eyes and drew a deep breath. Her musky scent filled his senses, and heat seared a path to his balls. God, there was something so sweet about her. Something that always crawled into his heart when he looked at her. Touching her, feeling her, making her come...it went beyond any feeling of joy Max had ever known.

He looked up and caught her gaze. Without breaking eye contact, Max leaned forward and licked her outer lips. Juice flowed from her sex. Sweet as honey and hot as sin, the taste of her sent his heart beating out of control.

Next, he slipped his tongue inside, and the taste of her exploded in his mouth. Anna closed her eyes, moaning his name. He was certain he'd never get her taste or the sounds she made out of his mind.

Again and again, he thrust his tongue inside, licking, slurping her cream. Max moved up and took her swollen clit into his mouth as he slid two fingers into her slick channel.

Juice wet his fingers as her inner muscles clamped tight around them. He continued to tease her clit while he added another finger. Her moans grew louder, her muscles constricted around his fingers. Planting her feet on the bed, she pushed against his mouth. Max knew she was close, straining to reach the top. Humming, he sucked on her clit. Anna exploded, her convulsions shaking her body, and he lifted his head. Her hair was a mass of curls around her head, her mouth open in a silent moan. Max had never seen anything so beautiful in his life.

He moved up her body, licking each nipple on his way. Capturing her mouth in a searing kiss, he thrust his cock in her to the hilt with a fast, hard push. Her muscles still quivered with her orgasm, pulling him deeper, testing his control. Lifting his upper body, he rested his weight on his hands.

So completely lost in her, the taste of her still in his mouth, he plunged one, twice, and on the third thrust, Anna moaned out his name as he felt her sex clamp tight around his shaft. Max followed her into bliss after one more drive into her heated core. She shivered as her inner muscles convulsed around his dick.

He collapsed, his body drained of any strength. A moment later, he gathered enough to roll to his side and pull her against him.

Anna purred. There was no other way to describe the sound. "Well, you're right about that, Max. I feel even better now."

He chuckled and squeezed her closer. His eyelids grew heavy as he relaxed and his thoughts drifted to the edge of consciousness.

But somewhere in the back of his mind, something nagged. Anna was a woman used to variety, keeping her relationships light. Max didn't relish being another idiot she dumped. He'd known for years she kept herself at a distance with men to protect herself. He had to overcome whatever it was that made her run away from serious relationships.

Panic rose in his chest, almost clogging his throat. With sheer force of will, he batted it away. Why had it become so important to keep her in his life? Anna had always been there, a temptation just out of his reach. But now that he'd had her, Max knew deep down in his soul he could never give her up. Seeing her every day, knowing she was off-limits. Max had claimed her and she was now his. Somehow, he'd convince her that they were meant to be together.

His thoughts drifted to possible ways to plead his case, all of them involving Anna naked. His lips curved as he drifted to sleep with that thought, knowing that in the morning, she would understand this was more than a one-month fling. If not, convincing her would definitely be worth his while.

ꙮ

Anna pulled her comforter closer and snuggled deeper in her bed. Normally, she was an early riser. She loved to hop out of bed and greet each day. Attacking her chores, at home and at work, wasn't always her favorite thing to do. But she loved the fact that she was in charge of her life, professional and personal. She'd succeeded where many thought she would fail with her restaurant, and each day she took personal satisfaction that she proved all the naysayers wrong. Even if there was some gossip about Brad's behavior, it would die soon. And no matter what happened yesterday, it was a brand-new start in the morning.

Even so, it was hard to get out of bed when her dreams were delightfully delicious. All of them revolved around Max, naked. It was as if she could feel his breath against her skin, know what it was like the moment he slipped inside of her and the way he looked when he came. She shifted her butt around, trying to ease the ache created by the fantasy, and came in contact with a wall of hard, muscled skin.

Anna froze. The memories of the previous night washed over her, tumbling in one on top of the other through her mind. A fire lit her blood. Tasting him, feeling him, having his mouth on hers, on her flesh, on her sex...

*Holy shit.*

Max was in her bed. She'd been sober enough to remember falling asleep with her head on his chest, the steady beat of his heart lulling her to sleep. But the reality of Max snuggled against her back sent panic racing through her. Jesus, what had she done?

Okay, Anna knew what she'd done. She'd slept with the one man she shouldn't have slept with. Max was okay to lust after secretly, in her dreams, but she couldn't handle him in her bed. He was reserved for her fantasies because having him in her life was more important than a fling. If she let him into her bed again, it could ruin their friendship. Anna just hoped it hadn't been damaged by her actions last night.

She closed her eyes again and swallowed. Every caress, every lick, every little sigh replayed in her mind. Anna had never been a prude about sex, but last night, Max tilted the axis of her preconceived notions about men. She'd suspected Max would be good in bed. But given the women he'd dated in the past, including Cynthia, she had been positive Max would be bland in his sexual tastes. She shivered. He was anything but.

He'd been into control. She could tell it was a preference for him. And she had expected it, but not to the extremes he'd exercised over her. The way he performed in bed, and out, made her think he might enjoy a little bondage. And Anna didn't like controlling men. Really, she didn't.

*Yeah,* her bitchy inner voice said. *Then why are your nipples getting hard just thinking about it?*

She shifted again. His arm snaked around her waist, anchoring her to him. His hardened shaft prodded the cleft between her ass cheeks.

"If you don't quit moving around, Anna, you'll make us both late." His rough morning voice curled around her, into her heart.

"Hmmm." It was all she could say. Anna couldn't think of anything else, because she was thinking it would be nice to be late for once. To spend all morning snuggled against Max's big, warm body.

"But then again, I don't have any meetings until after ten, so that should give us a few hours." His voice had deepened, and his shaft grew harder against her bottom. All her thoughts dissolved as his hand slid across her stomach, and then between her legs. He parted her lips and two fingers dipped inside her.

Already wet, another gush of liquid filled her sex. As Max continued to thrust his fingers in and out, he rubbed his erection against the cleft between her buttocks. Anna really shouldn't allow him to distract her. She knew they were destined for disaster if they continued, but as his lips nibbled her earlobe, she forgot her arguments.

"Max."

"Hmmm." His mouth vibrated against her lobe and she shivered. He moved from her ear, back to her neck, nipping at her skin, then licking. "We've got time."

"But I have to get to the restaurant."

"Why? You don't usually open on Friday mornings, do you? Usually Steve and John open, don't they?"

*Dammit*, she wasn't used to her lovers actually knowing her habits. And knowing Max, he had her schedule down pat with that computer brain of his.

"Yes, but..."

She lost her ability to talk as his fingers slid out of her sex and he moved down her back, placing kisses along the line of her spine. Her blood thickened and her pulse doubled. The man had a lethal tongue.

"But what, Anna?" he said against her skin.

*Oh God.*

As Max continued down her back, his hands slid to her hips, and he rolled her over.

Anna looked up at him, his hair disheveled, his jaw dark with a day's worth of whiskers, the sexy smile curving his lips, and her heart slid to her stomach. Lord have mercy, she wanted this. Anna wanted Max in her bed, in her life, in her heart forever.

This was *not* good.

No way was this anything she should be feeling. Men, even Max, didn't think of forever when they thought of Anna. Hot, steamy sex, no commitments; that was Anna Dewinter. There would be no happily ever after.

Her thoughts must have shown on her face because his smile faded. His lips turned down in a frown. He leaned closer, placing a hand on each side of her head. "Anna, is something wrong?"

His voice washed over her like a physical caress. The panic clawing at her stomach eased. Max rested his weight on one elbow and ran the backs of his fingers along her jaw. The tenderness in the action and darkening of his eyes shifted through her, sending a rush of warmth flooding her senses.

The sunlight, filtered through the blinds, cast a golden hue on his skin. Her breath tangled in her throat. Max was more than a man in good shape. He was a finely sculpted David. Of all the men she'd seen naked, she'd never witnessed such blatant male beauty.

Max would never be considered a pretty boy. He was much too hard for that, too serious. His crooked nose, the one she broke when she was six and he, ten, the strong dominant jaw, the thoughtful frown he usually wore, made him too powerful to be in that category. She'd always thought of him as a warrior.

"Anna?"

Anna swallowed. It would never last. She knew it. Max needed a woman like Cynthia, pleasant and quiet, with no strange piercings or tattoos. They lived in small-town Park City, Georgia. Conservative businessmen, even in the twenty-first century, didn't have wives like her. Outspoken and liberal to the core, Anna would never fit in at the functions he had to attend. She never had with her parents, and Anna knew she wouldn't with Max. And changing, well it would kill her. But she could push aside her reservations. Being with Max, living in the moment, would be enough, would have to be enough. Because if she wished for more, she'd end up with a broken heart.

She needed some distance. "That's a sweet idea, Max, but I need to get there early today. I'll hop in the shower. Coffee should be ready if you want to grab a cup before you go."

Anna slid out of bed and headed to the bathroom without looking back at him. With each step she had to battle the urge to jump back under the covers with him. To feel the warmth of his body next to hers, to give in to the need coursing through her body. No. She needed some space. If she climbed back on that bed, and back on Max, she'd probably never be able to let go. With that last thought, Anna closed the door behind her.

ꕥ

Max watched Anna's rounded ass disappear behind her bathroom door and sighed. There was definitely something cooking in that beautiful head of hers. The play of emotions that had come and gone over her face had held him momentarily enthralled. Anna could always hide her feelings from him, but this one time, he had seen them. Fear, then doubt, then sadness so deep he could feel it down to his bones.

He ran his fingers through his hair. Frustration, beyond the sexual, coursed through him. What to do? Anna would fight him if he confronted her. Or she would deny anything was wrong.

He'd watched her with men over the years and knew for a fact she liked them dancing to her tune. Max refused to be one of her typical conquests. Sexual conquest, that was different. But Anna felt she needed to control the timing of the relationship. Heck, she controlled the tenor of the relationship. Max had never seen her emotionally connect with any of her boyfriends.

No, Max needed to make her understand this was beyond what she was used to. Unfortunately, telling her would only result in her pulling further away from him. He'd have to show her. Loving Anna wouldn't be easy, but showing her would be tougher.

The sound of running water told him Anna was in the shower. The image of water trickling down her body, dripping from her nipples, sent a wave of heat straight to his dick. Max gritted his teeth and stood. That she could even think he would let her build a wall between them irritated him to no end. Max desperately wanted to grab her and shake her. Instead, he would love her body, heart and soul. He would show her in deed how much he needed her. How much she needed him. Taking a calming breath, he walked to the bathroom.

It was about time Anna learned he was around for keeps.

# Chapter Five

Anna allowed the cool water to slide over her body, hoping it would relieve her fevered skin. Every molecule in her being urged her to join Max back in her bed, to submit to the need pulsing in her veins. Anna accepted that last night was probably a fluke, a one-time...okay three-time thing. It was stupid, not to mention dangerous to her emotional well-being, to get used to it. Giving into the urge to snuggle would just make it that much harder to let him go when he was ready to leave.

She sighed and picked up her lilac-scented soap, enjoying the crisp clean scent. Even as she tried to think of other things, other distractions, she knew it was useless. Nothing was going to help. Ice-cold water, thinking about her ninth-grade algebra teacher...nothing turned her off when Max was lounging in her bed.

*Her bed.*

She closed her eyes. She would never forget the feeling of waking up next to him. His heat warming her, the scent of his aftershave mingling with her perfume, along with a heavy dose of passion that still clung to the sheets. Just thinking about it had her nipples so tight they ached. Anna soaped one breast, then the other, trying to relieve the tension. All the action did was cause more friction.

"Do you need any help?"

Anna gasped and looked over her shoulder. Max held her shower curtain in one hand as he leaned against the tiled wall. She'd been so distracted by her thoughts she hadn't heard the bathroom door open. His sexy smile deepened as his gaze traveled down her body, then back up, lingering on her ass. Every nerve ending tingled. All he had to do was look at her, smile and Anna was ready to jump his bones. Lord, she was really pathetic.

But the truth was, she didn't care. The heat coursing through her overrode her better judgment. No one could make her feel the way he did when his chocolate-brown eyes darkened. Her pulse accelerated, her nipples tingled, a gush of liquid wet the lips of her sex. Anna glanced down and saw his cock, hard and ready.

She met his eyes and offered him a smile.

"If you don't mind scrubbing my back, darling." Anna exaggerated her southern accent.

Max chuckled. Deep, sexy, the sound had her pulse scrambling. He stepped into the tub behind her. "I think I can help with a lot more than that." The dark promise in his voice sent another thrill racing along her skin.

He grabbed the soap from her and stuck his hands under the shower water.

"Jesus! You need some warm water, Anna."

"Wuss." She turned the knob further to the left. When she straightened, Max stepped closer to her, his shaft rubbing against the small of her back. He began at her shoulders, massaging and gliding his hands over her tense muscles.

"What's got you all uptight?" His breath warmed her ear. She shivered.

"Oh, nothing much. I'm just standing in the shower, with a six-foot-plus stud behind me. I have absolutely nothing to worry about."

"I'd think that would have the opposite effect."

She snorted as his hands slipped down her back, then over her hips. He skimmed them across, cupped a cheek in each hand, squeezing her aroused skin. His finger traced the cleft between her buttocks and she sighed in pleasure. The combination of his talented hands and the slick soap scattered her thoughts. A moment later, his hands were on her breasts. Max teased her nipples, pulling and pinching them as he ground his cock against her bottom. Anna's knees almost gave way as his fingers then eased down past her stomach to her sex. She placed her hands on the tile to steady herself. Her head spun, her body throbbed.

Wet and slick, his fingers slipped inside her. As Max thrust his fingers in and out, he barely touched her clitoris. Each little brush of his thumb pushed her closer to the edge but not enough to get her over. The tension in her drew tighter, her body quivering with the need to explode. He kept his touch light enough to titillate, but not enough for her to find satisfaction.

When she tried to push against his hand, Max chuckled.

"Patience, Anna. It's much better if you draw it out."

At that moment, he brushed his thumb against her clitoris again, and she growled. Frustration and irritation combined, heightening her senses. Her blood raced through her veins, heating her from within.

"Maxwell."

"I know I'm in trouble when you use my full name."

Max massaged her breast while he continued to torture her with his other hand. Her juices poured over his hand as her arousal grew. The pressure built, tension drew tighter. Before

Anna could break free, Max moved away from her, sitting down in the tub, pulling her on top of him. Anna sat facing him, straddling his lap.

"Shit."

The frustration in his voice was unmistakable. Max reached outside the tub and retrieved a condom. After ripping it open, he threw the wrapper aside and rolled it on. A moment later, Anna was sliding down his hard shaft. He held her hips, digging his fingers into her skin. The water sluiced over them as he set the rhythm, slower than she wanted.

She opened her mouth to protest, but he took one turgid nipple into his mouth, sucking and nipping. Heat surged through her blood. She moaned instead of complaining as his teeth scraped over the end of one nipple. Her every thought centered on the feel of his shaft thrusting into her, his tongue twirling around the tip of her nipple. The pressure built, the need to reach the pinnacle consumed her every action. Her stomach muscles tightened and quivered.

His hands moved from her hips to her hair, tangling in the mass of wet curls, pulling her down for a kiss. His tongue immediately thrust past her lips. She increased her speed as her tongue danced with his.

God, nothing had ever tasted as good as Max in the morning. Sensual, decadent, the flavor of him slid through her. His hands clenched tighter in her hair and he threw back his head, moaning her name. The sight of him in the throes of his orgasm drove her over the edge. Anna exploded, her inner muscles clamping around his shaft, pulling him deeper. His fingers dug into her flesh, but she barely noticed. Every muscle in her body quivered as her release swept over her.

Moments later, Anna collapsed against him. Max grunted and relaxed against the back of the tub. He pushed the mass of heavy curls away from her face and kissed her forehead. The tender action was almost her undoing, but the words she'd wanted to say for the past ten years stuck in her throat. Even men who liked to cuddle didn't appreciate declarations of love—no matter how good the sex was.

When she spoke, Anna deliberately kept her tone light. "I think I'll hire you, if that's what you call a back scrub."

His chuckle echoed in the bathroom and Anna bit back the disappointment as she stifled her emotions. It did neither of them any good wishing for things that would never happen.

ഇ

Later that morning, Max walked down the hall to his office, his step a bit lighter than usual. He'd stopped by his house on the way to work for a shave and a change of clothes, but his shower with Anna earlier occupied his thoughts. Each time Max replayed how it felt to slip into her warm, moist body, all the blood he had in his brain rushed to his dick.

There was still a lot to resolve with Anna. She didn't trust men. Sometime in her senior year in high school, something had gone wrong. She'd changed. It hadn't been just the typical young woman moving into adulthood changes, but one that turned her slightly more cynical than a lot of women her age. He'd seen it in her expression, the way she dealt with men. And, being a typical man, he'd never really asked. She'd shied away from any questions like that just as she did the night before. He had her trust on one level, but she didn't trust him beyond being friends. It would take a lot to convince her to have faith in him. But he was the man for the job.

By the time Max reached the door to his outer office, he was whistling. He'd passed a few people who did a double take as they walked by. Maxwell Chandler didn't walk down the hall with a smile on his face. He chuckled to himself. Max hadn't felt this good in...well...forever. It was as if he could do no wrong, and nothing bad would happen.

He opened the door, stepped into his outer office and stopped cold in his tracks. There on the sofa, dressed to the hilt in a pink linen suit, every blonde hair in place and her nose buried in a tissue, sat Cynthia.

She jumped up the moment he walked through the door. "I need to talk to you, Max."

Max looked at his secretary Jeanine, who rolled her eyes. She'd been in charge of contacting the country club and the caterers to work out the reneging on the contracts for the wedding, so she knew what had happened yesterday. He got the idea from her joy in the act that Jeanine hadn't been that happy with his selection of brides. He was beginning to wonder if anyone had been.

He glanced at his watch. "Okay, but I have a meeting soon, so it will have to be short."

Cynthia smiled and glided past him. Max didn't know what she wanted, but he knew it couldn't be good.

As he followed her into his inner office, the scent of her perfume left him feeling slightly nauseated. He preferred Anna's lilac soap.

"What do you want, Cynthia? I have a full day ahead of me." And, if there was a God, a full night of loving Anna.

Cynthia shifted from one foot to the other, then set her purse on his desk. She glanced past him. He glanced back and saw Jeanine peeking around the corner. He bit back a chuckle and shut the door in her face. Her aggravated sigh could be heard through the door.

"Now, tell me what you want."

Her lips turned up in that practiced smile of hers that irritated him.

"Well, after thinking about it, Max, I've decided that maybe I was a little too hasty when I called off our wedding yesterday."

# Chapter Six

Max stared at Cynthia and blinked. Did she say what he thought she said?

"What do you mean?" His voice was rougher than he intended. Damn woman. He didn't need this kind of aggravation.

Cynthia's smile faltered. "Just what I said. I want to get back together."

He bit back the growl threatening to erupt from his throat. "But...I *don't*."

Now her lips turned down and her blue eyes shimmered with unshed tears. Max sighed. He didn't want to hurt her, but after the previous night, nothing could keep him from Anna. Not Cynthia changing her mind. Not the ruckus canceling the wedding would cause. Not even Anna herself would keep Max from possessing every inch of her sweet body and heart.

But first, he had to clear up this mess. And, because it was mainly his creation since he'd proposed in the first place, he reminded himself to keep his voice calm. Cynthia had just had second thoughts, or she was smoking crack. Either way, loud noises and big arm movements scared her and extended the time he had to deal with her.

"Cynthia, I thought you had decided you didn't want to marry me. You said that very thing at lunch yesterday."

"Yes." She looked away nervously then apparently gained an ounce of gumption and met his gaze. The determination was there, but he could tell her heart wasn't in it. If so, she wouldn't have looked so sad. "But, then I tried to call you last night, and you didn't answer your home or cell phone. I left several messages. Where were you?"

Max didn't answer the question because he didn't even want to go there. He didn't feel guilty about Anna, but he also didn't want to slap Cynthia in the face with another woman, especially Anna. He motioned toward one of the chairs situated in front of his desk. After setting his briefcase down, he settled himself in his chair behind the desk and waited for her to continue.

"I...I tried to tell Daddy last night, but when I did, he became angry."

She sniffled into her tissue. If he thought she truly had changed her mind, he'd feel badly, but he had a feeling there was something else to it.

"Cynthia, you don't want to marry me."

Her head shot up and a look of mortification passed over her face. It was quickly followed by fear. Jesus, something bad must have happened.

"But he threw a fit." She visibly swallowed and her fingers tightened on the tissue she held. "I-I've never seen him quite that angry before. I mean, you know Daddy, he has a really bad temper, but he usually keeps it under lock and key."

No, he didn't, but Cynthia didn't do business with her father. He was known for being ruthless and vindictive. Chandler Industries did business with him because they needed his transportation services, but since Max took over from his father, there had been much discussion of switching to someone else. Until he threw his daughter at Max.

Max had been pretty sure her father never really took it out on Cynthia. The bastard was probably to blame for Cynthia's low self-esteem. But something cold slid into his stomach when he looked at the terror Cynthia exhibited. "Cynthia, your father didn't do anything to hurt you, did he?"

She shook her head and blew her nose in the most unladylike manner. He would have smiled if he didn't think she'd take it the wrong way.

"No. He said he would cut me off if I didn't marry you."

This wasn't going to be easy. Cynthia had little to no skills. She had a degree in something like art design, but had never really worked a day in her life. Just like her mother, Cynthia had been groomed for life as an executive's wife. It was practically medieval. And that probably made him a bastard because he should have thought about the woman he was marrying. He should have had some kind of thought to her personal and professional life beyond him. Truth was, she had no means of supporting herself.

"I sympathize with the position you're in, Cynthia, but I'm not going to marry you. You broke it off and I've...changed my mind."

He couldn't help the smile curving his lips as images of his morning shower with Anna flashed in his mind. Just thinking about sliding his hands across her wet skin sent his blood racing to his groin. Max shifted in his chair to relieve the tightness of his pants.

Cynthia's eyes narrowed, and the tears mysteriously disappeared.

"Where were you last night?" Accusation threaded her voice.

Irritation inched down his spine. Max didn't like to be questioned, and he really didn't care for her tone. She'd lost the right to question his whereabouts when she'd tossed up his ring at a lunch for which he paid.

"I really don't think that's any of your business, Cynthia."

She crossed her arms beneath her breasts. "I'm your fiancée. I think I have every right to know where you were last night."

Max leaned forward, placing his forearms on the desk. "Cynthia, we broke up yesterday. You said you didn't want to get married to me. You are no longer my fiancée."

Cynthia blinked, probably because she wasn't used to his harsh tone. He'd always used a gentle tone with her because he didn't want her to start crying.

Damn, but he dodged a bullet yesterday.

"But I changed my mind, Max." Cynthia smiled tentatively, apparently unsure of his reaction.

"But I haven't. I don't want to get married anymore."

Not to her. To Anna—now that was another thing. As soon as the thought popped into his mind, he knew the rightness of it. Max wanted Anna forever. Not just for a night, or a month, or even for a year. He wanted marriage and kids and the whole nine yards. Somewhere in his subconscious he must have known that, or he would have never gotten in bed with her. By taking that action, Max knew he'd meant forever. His heart smacked against his chest. He'd known he loved her but he had no idea it was past friendship and lust. It had evolved into the all-encompassing connection that could bring a man to his knees. He didn't like it one damned bit, but he didn't think there was much he could do about it. No, there was one thing to do about it. He was going to ensure he would have Anna in his bed and in his life from this point forward.

The problem would be convincing Anna.

"Max?"

He shook his head to clear his thoughts and refocused on the subject at hand and the woman giving him an assessing look.

"What?"

She sighed and rolled her eyes. He realized it was a common reaction he'd gotten from her over the last few months. It hadn't been that good of a match if she was already irritated with him before the wedding.

"I *said* Daddy was furious and is insisting on a wedding."

He settled back in his chair, comfortable with this subject. "Oh, well, he can insist all he wants. We will not be getting married. I like you, Cynthia, but you don't want to marry me any more than I want to marry you."

She opened her mouth to argue, but Max cut her off before she could utter a word.

"No. We can still do business. I have no problem with that. I told you and I will tell your father, I don't want to get married."

Her shoulders slumped and she sighed. He regretted his harsh tone. Despite everything, Cynthia wasn't a bad person; she'd just never done anything against her father's wishes. She was weak and unsure of herself. Max understood how scary something like this was for her. And although he understood and pitied her for her life, it didn't mean he would spend his married to her.

"Listen, we had those tickets to Bermuda for next week. Why don't you take yours and go have a good time? Figure out what you want to do, and then, if your father is still giving you trouble, I'll talk to him."

Cynthia nodded, her perfectly lined lips turned down in a frown. "I guess if I can't change your mind..."

"Cynthia, you don't want to change my mind."

"I guess I better go pack. Daddy said he'd call you to straighten it all out. But it won't be until later, since he just left for New York."

"Okay." Max took her hand, waited for her to stand and led her to the door. "I'll take care of it and you avoid his calls. By the time he gets back, he'll have cooled off and seen the rightness of our decision. And even so, it will be another week before you return. That will give him more time to settle his temper and accept that we're not getting married."

She kissed his cheek, then opened the door and left without a word. He thought about calling her father in New York himself, but he had other things to do first.

"I could ruin your life, you slam the door in my face again."

Max turned and laughed. Jeanine's blue eyes narrowed and she frowned. She'd been his father's secretary, knew more about the company and how to run it than Max and maybe even his father.

"Jeanine, you know better than to eavesdrop on the boss."

She leaned back in her leather chair, the one he'd gotten her for her last birthday, and gave him an evil smile. "You should know better than to piss off the secretary."

He cocked his head to one side as if considering her comment. Then, he straightened and nodded. "Yeah, I should." He allowed the slow, satisfied smile that he had every time he thought about the night before curve his lips. "But then, I'm learning to take chances."

Max left Jeanine with her mouth hanging open and stepped into his office to start making plans. He needed to make sure that everything was perfect, and that by the end of the "four-week factor", Anna understood how much she meant to him. A plan would help him control the situation. As long as he was the one in control, everything would move smoothly and work out just fine.

ꟈꟈ

Anna looked down at the figures on the spreadsheet and tried to concentrate. But for the fifth time in as many minutes, her thoughts wandered back to Max. The way he smiled at her, the way he looked at her when he knew she was full of bullshit, the way it felt as he shoved his—

"You must be thinking about something very naughty."

The object of her thoughts stood in the doorway of her office, that sinful smile curving his lips. Every nerve ending bounced to attention and saluted. Anna repressed the shudder of need rolling through her. She doubted Max was the type who would go for an office quickie.

This was so not good. Not good at all. Lust, passion, that was fan-fucking-tastic. But this overwhelming need to possess, to be possessed in return, was a bad, bad idea. Like right at this moment. She'd love for him to take her on her desk, the bustle of her business sounding just beyond the closed door. She cleared her throat and tried to clear her mind of the image of Max naked in her office.

"What's going on?" She kept her tone as light as possible.

Max shrugged. That enigmatic smile deepened as he stepped into the room and shut the door behind him. With long, deliberate strides, he walked to her desk, grabbed her hand and yanked her out of the chair. His arms enveloped her, pulling her closer, his hands resting on her ass.

Bending his head, he brushed his lips against hers.

"I just thought I'd stop by and see if you wanted to catch a movie tonight."

That sounded suspiciously like a date, and Anna didn't date. Not really. She needed an alternative or he would get suspicious. But, she couldn't come up with anything. Thinking had become difficult since he showed up in her doorway, and was getting harder by the minute as his talented fingers slid over her ass.

Clearing her throat, and hopefully her thoughts, she asked, "How about I pick up that new Tom Hanks movie that came out on DVD and we watch it at your place?"

Max didn't say no, but Anna could feel his disappointment. She almost gave in, said she'd do it. She didn't like the feeling of disappointing him. Something in her wanted to make him happy, to bring out that sexy smile. But she fought the need, the want to please him because she hadn't done that for a man since she was in high school. Before her heart could talk her mind into it, he gave her rear end one more soft caress then pulled away.

"Okay, but if we order pizza, just plain, nothing freaky like pineapple."

She sighed. "You are such a simpleton when it comes to pizza."

"Damn straight. Meat, cheese, what the hell else does a guy need? Seven o'clock?"

She nodded, and a moment later, he was out the door. Rolling her shoulders, she tried to ease away the uneasiness that had settled beneath her skin. She was playing a dangerous game being involved with Max. Anna would have to remember that despite the fact that Max tended to have long, serious relationships, she knew just what to expect out of men. Because she enjoyed sex, most men thought she was easy, but

Anna didn't sleep with every man she met. And when she did, she knew where to draw the line. No commitments. Men, especially a man like Max who liked to be in charge of most situations, didn't like to keep an assertive woman around.

Now each time he smiled at her like that, she needed to remind herself that it was sexual attraction, passion, lust. If Anna could prevent her heart from being involved she would be able to survive this affair. But, somewhere in the back of her mind, Anna worried she'd already passed that point. Her heart had been involved for over ten years.

Anna didn't like it, not one freaking bit. But, she thought as she collapsed back in the chair, she didn't know what to do about it.

# Chapter Seven

With a sense of satisfaction, Max lit the last few candles he'd placed around the dining room. Barry White, one of Anna's favorites, crooned softly in the background. He had everything ready, everything set to a T for her tonight. She wouldn't know what hit her. The woman actually thought she could keep him at a distance. He shook his head.

Max knew she thought going out constituted a date. She never dated any of her little boys. He'd see them around, but rarely did she go to a restaurant or a movie with them. Max, unless he was dating someone, was her go-to guy for functions. Business affairs mainly where both of them had contacts to keep up with. But, until today, they'd usually hit the newest comedies that were out because their sense of humor was so similar, and Max tended to date women who didn't get the movies he wanted to see. The thought of taking someone like Cynthia to *The Big Lebowski* was mind-boggling.

So, he was sure in Anna's mind she'd decided to avoid anything like a movie with him now that they were involved. That would be a date, and that would mean they were serious. They were. Anna just didn't know it yet. It was an aggravating and damn near embarrassing situation.

He sighed as he wondered why he had to love such a contrary woman. He wandered back into his kitchen to make the final preparations. Anna had had a lot of boyfriends—no strike that—lovers. She'd never really had a steady boyfriend. Well, there was Freddy What's-his-name in high school, but since then she'd never stayed with one guy long enough to consider him her boyfriend. It must have ended badly. But, he couldn't really remember her ever saying anything, or hearing anything. He'd been in college, but in small towns gossip always made the rounds two or three times. Especially with a woman as visible as Anna.

He chose a nice Merlot, setting it on the counter while he looked for the corkscrew. Max knew what the problem was with Anna and all her lovers, her boy toys. He'd bet his left nut that not one of them had ever tried to romance her. Hell, when he'd been in his early twenties he couldn't think past his dick either. If a woman, a little older, more experienced like Anna, had paid attention to him, Max was sure he would've been consumed with sex. Hell, he was in his thirties and it was taking over most of his thoughts. At least he was old enough now to be able to function, even with the lack of blood in his brain. Back then, though, if a woman didn't push, he didn't bother with any sort of courtship.

But this was different. This was Anna and she was for keeps. He knew men took her attitude for granted and thought she didn't want, or worse, deserve to be romanced. Anna's sexuality was out there for everyone to see. She didn't flaunt it, but it was unmistakable in her every move. She oozed sensuality. There were times he watched her walk across the room to him and every other person disappeared. The familiar shot of heat spread throughout his body. His dick twitched at just the thought of being with her, touching her, tasting her.

The doorbell rang, crashing into his thoughts. Max shook his head and took a deep breath, trying to control his libido. His plan was simple. He would force Anna to deal with him as a lover—boyfriend—not some sexual toy. She kept men dancing to her tune. Max knew she did that to protect herself. To win her heart, he had to take it to the next level. They knew each other better than Anna knew most of her lovers. Intimacy, not sex, was what she shied away from.

With that resolved he opened his front door and promptly lost every rational thought in his mind. There stood Anna, her hair pulled into a loose bun of curls atop her head, her lips painted cherry red, dressed in a loose, white cotton dress. With the fading sun behind her, every inch of her—her nipples, her bellybutton, her sex—was visible through the thin fabric. Anna wasn't wearing a stitch beneath the dress.

All remaining moisture in his mouth dried up, his balls tightened and his heart skipped a beat.

"Max?" Sensuality laced her voice and helped drain a bit more blood from his brain.

"What?"

He couldn't take his eyes off her nipples. A slight breeze tightened the fabric against her skin. He licked his lips.

"Max, you gonna let me in?"

He could hear the smile in her voice. He looked up and saw the amused satisfaction dancing in her eyes.

Heat slid through him, sending his pulse racing. When her words finally registered, he realized he was standing there staring at her like some horny sixteen-year-old. Swallowing hard, Max stepped back. Anna brushed by him, her fingers sliding over his free hand. The scent of her—wildflowers and musky woman—surrounded him, enticed him. When he raised his hand to scrub his face, it shook. Every cell in his body screamed for relief, for him to grab her, strip her out of that damn dress and plunge his cock deep inside her wet, hot sex.

Max drew in a calming breath and shut the door, resting his head against the cool wood. Most of the blood had drained from his brain, but he fought those primitive urges. Even if there was a good chance he might end up rolling on the floor and howling like a dog. She'd done this to show him that lust was all their relationship was about. The action was telling. On one hand, he was furious with her because she was trying to maintain the kind of relationship Anna had with all her little boy toys.

But, at the same time, his heart warmed at her attempt to throw him off-kilter. Going to such extremes might mean she felt threatened in some way. And the only thing that bothered Anna was showing the soft underbelly of her personality. Hard as a rock on the outside, she had a tender heart.

He followed her into his living room, enjoying the sway of her hips, the nearly transparent fabric showing every inch of her rounded ass. His fingers itched to slide beneath the material, skim the supple skin just under the fullest part of each cheek, then back up to the small of her back and her tattoo.

Dammit. Max took a deep breath as she started to turn to face him. The same little smile curved her lips. Anger and determination tightened his gut. Lust, passion, whatever she wanted to call it, would not be enough to make this work. He knew for a fact there was more to her feelings than sexual need. He mentally rubbed his hands together as he thought of the night lying ahead of them. If Anna thought this was some kind of battle, let the games begin.

ꙮ

Anna's body sizzled from the top of her head down to the tips of her cherry red toenails. More than once, she mentally kicked herself for choosing the dress she had. Lord, she'd worn the dress to push Max over the edge, but it had the same effect on her. Each time she moved, the full skirt slid against her overly sensitized skin. She'd been aroused when she showed up at the door. Since arriving, Max hadn't touched her. He didn't have to. The look in his eyes when he'd answered the door had sent her senses spiraling out of control, her body craving to scratch an itch. He'd kept his distance all night, avoiding her hands when she'd tried to touch him, even in the most casual of ways. It'd made her more determined, but he'd thwarted her every time.

As she crossed her arms over her aching breasts, she tried to think of something not related to Max, something nonsexual. But it wasn't working. First, he was standing in front of her smelling like a wet dream come to life. It didn't help that he'd dressed casually tonight. An old pair of button-down jeans hung on his lean hips, cupping his sex. The red polo shirt he wore was a size too small. It emphasized his well-defined chest and abs while highlighting the golden flecks in his chocolate-brown eyes.

"Would you like a glass of wine?" His resonant voice washed over her. She'd always loved the sound of his voice.

"Sure."

The moment he left her alone, she drew in a deep breath. The soft cotton fabric brushed against her nipples and she groaned.

"Is there something wrong?" He walked back into the living room, a glass of red wine in each hand.

"No, nothing's wrong."

Anna took a sip of wine to calm her nerves. Never in her life had she been this aroused. Especially considering that Max hadn't even touched her. Yet. The thought of his hands on her, skimming over her skin, sent sparks through her already overheated body. Liquid dampened the lips of her sex, and she fought the urge to squirm under his scrutiny.

"Are you feeling all right, Anna?"

She took another sip of wine.

"Of course."

Jesus, even Anna recognized the arousal vibrating in her voice. One side of his mouth kicked up knowingly. She should be really irritated that he found it amusing, but it turned her on more.

"Well, then we can go into the dining room. I decided to do something a little different tonight."

It was then the scent of garlic and tomatoes reached her. All she had noticed before was Max—the way he looked, the way he moved, the way he smelled.

When she stepped into the room, her breath tangled in her throat at the sight before her. The only light came from the multitude of candles he'd placed on every available surface. Barry White's smooth, rich voice sang in the background, and in the center of the table sat a pepperoni pizza from the local pizzeria.

The effort he went to shouldn't really charm her, but it did. The time he took, picking her favorite wine, her favorite music and serving pizza on china... It was just so *sweet*.

Something unfamiliar curled inside her heart, warming her from the inside out. She swallowed her panic. Max didn't think there was more to their relationship than sex. This was the way he was. He romanced every woman he was involved with. Lord knows she'd watched him do it plenty of times. She'd wondered how it felt to get that treatment, to be the focus of his attention.

And now, after years of watching and yearning, she knew. Delight shivered through her.

Was this what all the women before her felt?

For the first time ever she felt special, cherished. No matter how she tried to stomp it back, remind herself that it wouldn't last, it did no good. Lord help her, she didn't want it to end.

# Chapter Eight

"Why don't you take a seat?" Max asked, trying his best to keep his voice even. It wasn't easy, because he knew each time she moved, the fabric of her dress brushed against her nipples, arousing her.

She nodded. He pulled out the chair and she settled into it. Unable to resist, he leaned forward and kissed the top of her head. Before he could grab her by her hair and yank her down the hall to his bedroom, he stepped back and went to his chair.

They chatted about the people they knew, the local happenings, anything he could think of to draw his attention away from the those red lips, or the way her breasts swayed each time she moved. Damn, didn't she know what her going without a bra was doing to him?

Her lips curved as she took a sip of her wine.

Hell, yes, she did. *Minx.* He was trying to take this to the next level, but she wanted to keep it all sexual.

Thoughts of his plans, images of what he was prepared to do, tumbled through his mind. Max had to admit, he didn't play fair, either.

ꕥ

After dinner, they settled in the living room to watch the movie Anna had brought. She snuggled closer as Max slid his arm across her shoulders. He played with the sleeve of her dress, his fingers tickling her arm. With each brush against her skin, a jolt of electricity shot through her. He was playing some kind of a game that she was losing. If she didn't get a handle on what he was doing she would be on her knees begging him for sex. His fingers slid over her arm again. This time she couldn't suppress the shudder.

Fine. If that's what he wanted, so be it. Inwardly, she declared war and decided to intensify this battle. She rested her hand on the top of his leg. A moment later, she began to massage the inside of his thigh. Instantly, his muscles stiffened under her touch. She smiled to herself as she inched her fingers up his leg to the very top of his thigh. His breathing accelerated and deepened.

Just to be evil, she pretended interest in the movie while she moved her fingers in lazy circles within inches of his cock. Without looking, she knew he was hard. Just thinking about it sent another wave of heat rolling through her, urging her to move her hand higher. The need to touch him, to unzip his pants and take his cock in her hand, in her mouth...

She drew in a deep breath, trying to calm the need screaming through her. She wanted so badly to touch Max, to have him touch her, caress her skin, but her desire to teach him a lesson was more important.

As his arm slid from her shoulder to her waist, she held her breath. A moment later, his fingers inched up to the underside of her breast. Lightly, too lightly for her own satisfaction, he massaged her skin through the thin fabric of her dress. The action drew the material tighter across her nipples. Ever so slightly, he pulled on her dress, allowing the fabric to show the definite outline of her hardened nipple.

She gritted her teeth and moved her hand higher, barely touching his obvious erection. His hand stilled. Over and over, she brushed the back of her fingers against his cock. Out of the corner of her eye, she saw him swallow, hard. Even through the thick denim, she could feel the outline of his hardened shaft. To push him over the edge, she took one finger and, starting at the top, slowly slid down his cock.

She only got halfway down when he groaned and grabbed her hand. A minute later, she was turned upside down as he threw her over his shoulder and stood.

"Max!"

He smacked her ass. "Shut up. I swear, woman, you just don't know when to give up."

He strode down the hall to his bedroom. Anticipation snaked through her. She really shouldn't be turned-on by this Neanderthal attitude, but she couldn't deny the excitement coursing through her, causing her nipples to tighten further as more liquid gushed between the lips of her sex. There was definitely something exciting about a man who attacked in a good way.

A moment later, he dropped her on the bed. For the second time in as many days, he'd carried her, then thrown her on a bed like some kind of caveman. As a twenty-first-century woman, she should really be appalled. But there was no way to ignore the fact that every nerve ending in her body tingled. She craved Max just the way he was—dominating and aggressive.

Standing before her, he rested his hands on his hips, his nostrils flaring with each breath he took. Her gaze traveled down his body and she licked her lips when she saw his erection straining against his jeans. He stepped forward, and before she knew what he was doing, he grabbed the bottom of her dress and slid it up her body, allowing his fingers to brush her skin as he did. When he had it off her, he tossed it on the floor behind him. An instant later, he was stripping off his shirt, then practically ripping off his jeans. Her breath caught in the back of her throat when he was finally, gloriously, naked. Golden skin, defined muscle, Max had no competition in her mind. Before he could tackle her, she slipped from the bed and dropped to her knees in front of him.

Max looked down at Anna's bent head and almost came at the sight of her kneeling in front of him. The curls she'd fastened to the top of her head now lay about her shoulders in abandon. Their foreplay in the living room had been light, nothing compared to what he usually liked. He loved teasing, pushing a woman higher than she'd ever been before. But knowing Anna saw him as a challenge turned him on. Usually the initiator, Max found her brand of aggressiveness more arousing than sex with other women.

Every fiber of his being demanded she take him in her mouth, but he wanted her to call the shots. Allowing her to control the rhythm of their intimacy was pushing him beyond anything he had felt before. The thrill was knowing he was at her mercy. She cupped his balls with one hand, squeezing, caressing them, her nails scraping against the sensitive skin. They drew tighter and a drip of precum wet the head of his dick. As she continued to massage his balls, she curled the fingers of her other hand around the base of his cock.

She slid her hand up the length and back down. Blood drained from his head and rushed straight to his dick. His head spun as he watched her lick the cum off the tip with her tongue.

Closing her eyes, she licked her lips. "Max, you taste wonderful. The perfect dessert."

*Jesus.* She twirled her tongue around the top of his shaft, then took the crown of his cock into her mouth. Just enough to tease, not enough to satisfy. She circled the tip with her tongue again, and when he was sure he was ready to scream, she accepted the length of him into her warm mouth. She looked up, caught his gaze and slowly began sucking on him. She kept one hand on his balls, moving her fingers over them as she worked his cock in earnest. Each time she drew to the top of his dick, she passed her tongue over the head.

He threaded his fingers through her hair, molding his hands to her head. She closed her eyes, humming as she increased the speed of her ministrations. The vibrations reached down to his toes. He curled them into the carpet and gritted his teeth, trying to keep from losing all control.

"Oh, Anna, yeah, baby."

His muscles tensed as she pushed him further, massaging his balls, sucking and slurping his dick. When Max thought he would never find relief, when he was sure there was no way of feeling any better than he did at that moment, he exploded. Anna continued sucking as he came. She licked up one side and down the other as he gyrated his hips, fucking her mouth, knowing nothing had ever felt as good as this. Seconds later, they both collapsed on the bed and he pulled her close, reveling in the feel of her soft skin next to his.

"Well, Maxwell, I think I won that little game."

He chuckled. "Give me a minute, Anna, and we'll do round two."

# Chapter Nine

Max awoke to a small slant of sunshine warming his face, and he smiled, keeping his eyes closed. Drawing in a deep breath, he enjoyed the spicy scent of Anna, wildflowers and passion. He'd never be able to smell lilac and not think of how it felt holding Anna, slipping into her body, hearing her moan his name. After a week of nights spent learning Anna inside and out, Max knew he'd yet to completely get his fill of her—and never would.

Nothing felt as good as waking in Anna's bed. Well, okay, making love with Anna ranked ahead of that and falling asleep with her snuggled against him was probably a tie. But, there was definitely something to be said about Saturday morning snuggling.

Thinking of just what sort of snuggling he'd like to accomplish, he rolled over to pull her into his arms and found the bed empty. He opened his eyes and looked around the room. Sitting up, he listened for clues to where she might be. No water was running and her robe was lying over the foot of the bed. From the brightness of the sun filtered by the blinds, Max realized he'd slept later than he thought.

The panic that welled up, almost choking him, was completely irrational and embarrassing, but he couldn't stop it. Where the hell had she gone this time? he thought angrily as he grabbed a pair of jeans and put them on, zipping but not buttoning them. He stomped out of the room, irritated and aroused and wholly not in a good mood. He could smell the coffee she'd brewed and instead of going for a much-needed cup, he followed the sound of the birds chirping. She'd left her sliding glass door open. He found her sitting on her porch, sipping coffee and staring out over the lawn in deep contemplation.

Since she hadn't noticed him, Max felt free to study her. Her brow was puckered, her lips frowning and she looked as if she were trying to solve the problems of the world. He didn't like the expression on her face, the unhappiness he saw there. Not that he didn't think Anna wasn't given to deep thoughts. Unlike a lot of men, he never assumed she was dumb. Lord knew she made a killing with her restaurant because of her sound business decisions. No, this wasn't business weighing on her. And if it wasn't, his worry was that it was their relationship.

Uneasiness shifted through him as he watched her sip her coffee. It wasn't guilt, per se. Max knew he hadn't done anything in particular to hurt her but there was an air of pain settled around her. It hurt Max just to see the resigned look in her gaze. Prodding her to find out her worries would do no good and he'd end up irritated he couldn't get it out of her. She wouldn't open up to him about this.

He rubbed his hand over his chest, his concerns increasing as she sighed. The need to ease the worries, to keep her from pain, outdid his own basic need for acceptance. Making her happy, lessening her pain—those took precedence.

Anna relaxed against the back of her wicker chair and stared out over her back lawn enjoying the cool morning breeze as she sipped her coffee. Late May was one of her favorite times in South Georgia. The azaleas were growing like crazy since the heat of summer had not slapped them yet. Mornings were still comfortable enough to sit outside and watch the world awaken on a sleepy Saturday.

She'd snuck out to her back porch, leaving Max still asleep looking entirely too right in her bed. Since they'd become lovers less than a week ago, they hadn't spent a night apart. It was more than a little unsettling to realize she'd become so dependent on him. Not so much dependent, but maybe expectant. And expectations were dangerous things to have in an affair. Even something as simple as having him next to her in bed, the loss of that would be almost unbearable if she didn't keep it on the level. It'd cut her deeper than any other pain she'd been through.

"Serious thoughts on such a beautiful morning."

She turned and found the object of her thoughts standing at the sliding glass door. His hair was a mess as if he rose and immediately went looking for her. He was shirtless and wore only a pair of jeans, the top button unsnapped.

Trying to resist the temptation he offered on a regular basis, she turned her head, took a sip of coffee and looked back over her lawn. "Just thinking about my meeting with the real-estate agent yesterday."

It wasn't exactly true...okay she was lying through her teeth. But she didn't want to discuss anything on the relationship level. Max still thought more of their union due to his own sense of obligation. He hadn't come to terms with the situation.

"Hmm." He said nothing else and being a coward she didn't look at him as he settled into the chair next to hers. He stretched his long legs out, crowded her and then rubbed his feet against hers. “So, tonight we have the monthly dinner, but we have a whole day free to play.”

She did look at him then and frowned. “Dinner?”

He studied her and a look that might have been irritation came and went in his eyes so fast she was sure she’d been wrong. “Yes. The Lake City Chamber of Commerce dinner. We go every month together.”

Yes, but that was before...well, before.

“I wasn’t sure if I was going to go this month.”

This time, he didn’t try to hide his exasperation. “No. We made plans to attend.”

From the set of his jaw there would be no arguing with him. “Max, be reasonable. We can’t go to the dinner together.”

Now, he was watching her with that patient look that made her want to smack him. She knew it meant he was puzzle solving again.

“But we go every month. Or most months.” He waved the idea away. “It would look odd if we both showed up and didn’t sit together.”

She couldn’t argue with that. “Still, you know everyone has found out that you and Cynthia called it quits.”

“Yeah,” he said with a chuckle then took her coffee cup. He sipped, making a face. “Why do you put all that crap in it?”

“Crap? Creamer and sugar is crap?” She grabbed her cup back. “Get your own damn coffee.”

“But, then I would have to get up, and I’m too comfortable.”

The smile he offered her had a mix of innocent boy and wicked man. It struck a chord in her heart...her soul. A lump rose in her throat and she swallowed.

“Can we get back to the subject at hand?”

"And that would be..."

"Dinner," she said from between clenched teeth.

"Oh. What about it? I heard they're planning on the regular rubber chicken—"

"Max! I'm not talking about the dinner itself. I couldn't care less what they are serving us."

"Then why do you complain each month?" Max asked, his tone filled with amusement. She opened her mouth to blast him, but he stopped her by leaning forward and trailing his finger along her jaw. "Don't worry, Anna."

She wanted to tell him to shut the hell up, but the tender touch had her pulse scrambling and her mind going blank. Just as simple as that, the argument evaporated. She knew he still didn't understand, but she loathed to argue and watch the warm look drain from his gaze.

"Okay." She rose from her chair and took his hand. "How would you like to have a cup of coffee prepared by the owner of the premier coffeehouse in town?"

He stood, curling his fingers into her hand, and followed her into the living room. "I'd like it much better if I could have that coffee after making love to her."

The deepening of his voice vibrated down her spine. She sent him a slow smile as she looked over her shoulder at him, tightening her fingers against his. "Anything to please a customer."

ꟳ

"Are you sure you want to drive my car?" Anna asked, giving him a confused look as he took the keys from her limp fingers.

"Yes. What guy wouldn't?"

She glanced at him then shook her head and walked to the passenger side door. For a moment, he watched her, enjoying the sway of her hips beneath the smart business suit. Anna didn't always dress so conservatively. Well, if you could call a lipstick red suit that hugged every curve, and the thigh-highs he'd watched her don, conservative. But for some reason, she'd decided to drag out a suit she reserved for weddings.

He knew part of it had to do with her line of questioning earlier. Like going to a dinner would make anyone think they were sleeping together. Hell, if anything, the fact that their cars had been parked out in front of each other's houses over the past week all night long would be what tipped them off. Granted, he'd been busy at work dealing with contract negotiations that he hadn't paid much attention to what people were saying, or any looks he'd gotten.

He slid behind the wheel of her car and sighed.

"Oh, good lord, don't date my car, just drive it."

Her amused exasperation had him grinning. "Sorry, but there is no way I can just drive this lady. And please, don't call her an it."

She laughed as he started the engine. The sound of it was lost when the stereo blasted an ABBA song.

"Sorry," she shouted and turned it down.

He pushed her hand away and hit an oldies station playing Sam Cooke. "How can you play that disco crap in this car?"

"Because it's *my* car. *My* beautiful, vintage T-bird that you may drive and covet, but always know it is mine and I can do whatever I want in it."

He slid his arm along the back of her seat and reversed out of the driveway. "Hmm, that could lead me to some interesting suggestions." He waggled his eyebrows at her and put the car in drive.

"Max. Jesus, who would have known you were a nymphomaniac? Besides, you always try and drive boring cars. Even the color is boring. Do you think you could pick another color than tan or brown?"

As he shot past another car on the two-lane highway, Anna cussed.

"*Max*. Do you think maybe you should slow it down a bit?"

"Nope."

He accelerated, enjoying the feel of the evening air, dewy with the afternoon rain. The power of her car took hold and he tightened his hands on the wheel. Damn but he loved the car. Always had. She rarely let him—or anyone else—drive it. He'd loved it since he helped her pick it out two years earlier. He glanced over at Anna and noticed the frown of displeasure.

"I'm going the speed limit."

"No. You're not." She leaned forward to look at the dial. "You're speeding."

"I'm within five miles of the speed limit. That means I'm not really speeding."

When she didn't say anything for a few moments, he looked over at her again. She studied him like he was some sort of experiment gone bad.

"This isn't like you, Max. You usually go below the speed limit and you always pay attention to the road."

He glanced back at the road and saw the entrance for the convention center. Slowing down, he easily turned into the parking lot, then found a space up front. When he killed the engine, he noticed she was still staring at him suspiciously.

"What?"

"You aren't acting like yourself."

Without hesitating, he leaned forward, cupped the back of her neck with his hand and drew her closer to him. He brushed his lips over hers, then said, "Don't worry about it, Anna. I'm trying out all kinds of new things."

After he gave her another quick kiss, he got out of the car, hurrying to open the door for her. As she stepped out, he noticed Josephine Swanson was watching them. Next to her stood her son, the manager of their family-owned gym. Freddy Swanson, the one Anna had dated in high school. Rumor had it that he'd gone bankrupt in some business he'd started in Atlanta and had to beg for help from his family. He was eyeing them with lascivious interest that made Max want to go smack the bastard. When Anna noted his interest, she turned to the mother and son and smiled.

"Mrs. Swanson, Freddy. How are you two doing?"

Mrs. Swanson smiled at Anna, apparently unaware her son was giving Anna a little too much interest.

"Good evening, Anna. I see you two made it as usual. How are things at the restaurant?"

"Oh, they're fine." Anna shut the door and stepped up on the curb. "You should come in for the new lunch items. I have a gazpacho soup I know you would love."

The older woman patted Anna on the hand and started to walk away. When she noticed her son hadn't followed—mainly because he was inching toward Anna—Mrs. Swanson said, "Freddy, come on. I told you I wanted to make sure to get a good seat."

Max stepped up next to Anna. Freddy studied them, his gaze moving from Anna to Max, and then let himself to be led away by his mother. As he watched them walk away, Max noticed that Freddy glanced back at them a couple of times. An urge to stake his claim overtook Max's better judgment. He slipped his arm over Anna's shoulders and pulled her closer to him. She shot him a warning look, but he pretended he hadn't seen it and urged her to walk.

"Max."

She rolled one shoulder but he just held on tighter. It was asinine and damn near embarrassing but the look of interest Freddy had thrown her had sent Max almost into a panic. As they neared the door, she stopped. He glanced down at her and frowned.

"Just what the hell is the matter?" he asked.

From the look she sent him, it probably wasn't the best choice of questions.

"Hmm, not sure where I should start. From wanting to drive my baby, to acting like a Neanderthal on steroids, to the fact you are trying to get us through a doorway side by side when it isn't big enough, I am just not sure where to begin."

He glanced at the door, which was narrow, and realized that she had been right. Max also knew he'd been an ass in front of Freddy, so Max decided to pick the one thing he could defend.

"I don't see what is wrong with me driving your car."

She threw up her hands in disgust and wiggled away from him. Looking back over her shoulder as she walked through the door, she said, "Leave the gorilla act outside. I'm not in the mood to deal with the questions."

Her body vibrated with feminine indignation. He followed, knowing she was right, but not feeling any better as she turned the head of almost every man in the room. Max had never had this need, this amazingly overwhelming desire, to just smack every single one of them. Even old Mr. Phillips, a retired schoolteacher who Max knew was a flaming homosexual.

But, for Anna, he would calm the beast until they got out of there. Even if he felt like removing Freddy's arms and stuffing them down the bastard's throat. He would act civilized and professional. As he watched Freddy's gaze roam down Anna's back to her ass, accentuated in the short red skirt, Max bit back the growl—barely—and reminded himself that ripping the man's face off would be bad for his image, although the idea appealed to him greatly. Almost enough to make him forget good sense.

ഩ

Anna thought that she'd done her best to keep her anger from boiling over into work, which this dinner was, but every five minutes or so, Max did something that pissed her off. He was pushing all those buttons that she'd worked years to put out of commission. But for some damn reason, he picked tonight to become a pig.

"You know, dear, you should really just let the boy have his say."

She looked at Mrs. Walfren, the owner of a small dress shop in the same strip mall where Anna's restaurant was located. Anna knew that people were speculating, especially since Max was stomping around mad at the world. But she didn't want people to think they were going to be an item forever.

"Boy?"

The older woman smiled at her and glanced over her shoulder. She followed her gaze and found Max standing off to the side of the cash bar with a couple other men, watching her. She huffed then rolled her eyes, turning to face Mrs. Walfren again.

"So nice to finally see you two together."

Horrified she'd been right people would speculate on the change in their relationship, she tried to deny it, but even when she spoke she wasn't convinced. "We're not together."

"If not, Maxwell has designs on it. A man doesn't look at a woman like that and not at least want more."

Anna sighed, thoroughly irritated with Max for his behavior and herself for being somewhat aroused by it. It was nice to have a man show a little possessiveness.

"Well, we're not. We've always been friends, nothing more."

The older woman leaned forward and said in a confidential voice, "Truthfully, I was happy to hear Cynthia Myers had broken off the engagement. Those two weren't right. Now, you two, I think you'd be perfect."

"Mrs. Walfren, that's very nice of you, but we're too different."

Her pale blue eyes studied Anna for a moment or two, long enough to make Anna uncomfortable. "I've been in the business of making dresses for brides for over thirty years, dear. I was married for twenty-five of those years, and I have never in my life seen a man who wanted a woman more than that one over on the other side of the room."

"Wanting is different than being perfect for each other." As soon as she said the words, she winced, wishing she hadn't voiced her thoughts out loud.

"Anna, believe me, there is a lot more than wanting behind that look of his. If my own Harold had looked at me that way we would have had more than our eight kids."

Anna had just taken a drink and promptly choked. Trying to hold onto her dignity, she blotted her lips with her napkin and cleared her throat.

"But, there is so much you two have in common. Why, you practically grew up together. And just look how well you have always gotten along."

Not knowing what to say to dislodge the older woman's ideas, Anna thanked her and wandered outside to the patio that looked over the manmade lake behind the convention center.

She walked to the stone railing and closed her eyes, enjoying the warm, moist breeze. Thinking about Max, about their relationship, wouldn't do any good. Hopefully, they would get through the evening without embarrassing themselves too much. She'd just make sure before going out with him again that they had a discussion. With that decision made, her nerves a little more settled, she turned to go back into the dining room and came face-to-face with Freddy Swanson.

He offered her that damn cocky smile that used to make her sigh, but now just irritated her.

"Evening, Anna. Been a while, huh?"

# Chapter Ten

Anna looked at the boy she'd once thought was king and tried not to laugh. He was still attractive enough, she supposed. Tall, with the lean build of a swimmer, he'd always had a ready smile that hid his nasty behavior. With those sharp blue eyes, he'd seen more than she'd understood at the time of their...relationship. He'd known her vulnerabilities and how to use them to his advantage. For years after the entire mess, she'd felt the heat of embarrassment each time she saw him, or heard his name mentioned. But there was something missing now. The charm was there, but the luster of high-school prince was gone. When she'd heard he'd returned to Park City, she'd been a bit disappointed. Reminders of that time in her life weren't what she'd been looking for.

"Evening, Freddy."

He shook his head. "No one calls me that these days but my mother. My friends call me Fred."

"How unfortunate for you."

He chuckled good-naturedly, but she sensed a tension beneath the veneer. Something that had worry settling between her shoulders. She'd learned long ago just how nasty good-boy Freddy could get. She took a sip of her drink, not really tasting it, and attempted to come up with a way to leave graciously. She was pretty sure telling him to fuck off wouldn't be considered professional.

"Mom said you attend every month so I thought I would pop in and see how you've been."

Apparently ignoring his repeated phone calls at her restaurant hadn't explained her position to him. But then, boy kings usually didn't accept the truth if it bothered them. They liked their bubble world where people really cared they'd won the state championship ten years ago. Still, she would not make a scene.

"I've been well."

"I was wondering if you were free Friday night. I understand there's a new Italian restaurant that opened in Valdosta, thought you would want to pop in, catch up."

She couldn't find her voice to answer. This was the one guy in high school she mooned over, wanted and gave her virginity to. Then he tossed it all away, telling her she wasn't good enough for him. Now he thought they'd...date?

Before she could answer though, the sound of shoes scraping on the patio caught her attention. She didn't have to look to know who it was. Every sense went on alert from the amount of testosterone he was exuding as he walked toward her. When she could see Max's face, she knew from his dangerous look he'd heard Freddy ask her out. In the mood Max had been in, that could prove dangerous for Freddy's well-being. Wanting to avoid any kind of scene, she stepped around Freddy and up to Max.

"Max, you remember Freddy, don't you?"

Max's gaze moved from her to Freddy, his jaw twitching. Casually, he slipped his arm around her and turned her so she was standing next to him, both of them facing Freddy as a couple.

"Yeah, I think I do. You graduated with Anna, didn't you?"

When Anna saw Freddy's face she didn't laugh but it was a near thing. The ready smile dissolved into a scowl that resembled a three-year-old's pout. All his charming personality seemed dimmed when faced with Max's dominating nature.

"Yes, Anna and I graduated together. We did date for a while, also."

Anna glanced at Max to see how he took the news. One eyebrow rose and his lips curved in a smile that if Freddy were smart—which he wasn't—he would be wary of.

"Interesting. And I am assuming that she broke it off?"

"No. I believe it was mutual."

Mutual? Calling her easy and cheap, and saying he would never take someone like her to the prom, that was *mutual*? Jesus, she didn't want to know what a nasty breakup was like with Freddy. Max sensed her irritation, because his fingers moved over her shoulder as if to soothe her.

"Oh, then your loss. I guess." Max looked back over his shoulder. "I believe your mother's looking for you, Freddy."

Freddy shot Max a sour expression, then smiled at Anna. "I was thinking about popping into that little restaurant of yours this week."

She didn't say anything but nodded and with another irritated look at Max, Freddy left them in search of his mother. As soon as they were alone, Anna walked to the edge of the patio.

"Just what the hell was that about?"

"Now, Anna, I know you're mad at me, but—"

She turned and faced a chagrined Max, who apparently thought she was mad at him. “Not you.”

He looked nonplussed. “You’re not mad at me?”

Wasn’t that just like a man? Every little thing in her life was supposed to be about him. She settled her hands on her hips. “Listen, Max, the whole world doesn’t revolve around you. I do have other things I worry about. This is about Freddy.”

“Freddy?” His tone had turned downright grumpy, but she ignored it.

“First, asking me on a date, as if!” She crossed her arms over her breasts, her temper finally letting loose. “Then to say ‘your little restaurant’. The nerve. He went bankrupt and I’m opening another place. He had to come work for his parents because he couldn’t find a job anywhere else.”

There was a beat of silence as Max cocked his head and studied her. “So, you’re mad he asked you out and then belittled your business?”

She rolled her eyes. “Yes. I don’t really care about what he thinks, but I really resent that tone.”

His chuckle caught her by surprise. “Well, Freddy always was an asshole.”

She stared at him and then smiled. “Oh, but his friends call him *Fred* now.”

Max walked forward, the warmth she felt in her chest reflected in his eyes and the smile he offered her. “How unfortunate for him.”

She laughed at that. “Funny, I said the same thing.”

He cupped her face, and all that comfortable warmth shot to raw, sexual heat at the feel of his hands against her flesh. Slowly, he moved his thumb over her bottom lip.

“We can skip dinner.”

She shook her head, knowing he would do it. "I'm hungry even if it is rubber chicken."

He smiled and tilted her head up as he bent his toward hers. Softly, he brushed his mouth over hers. It was the briefest of touches, but her body was humming with need by the time he pulled back. He moved beside her, sliding his hand around her waist. Her mind was still spinning and her heart still melting from the tender kiss he'd given her. As they reached the opened double doors, he bent his head so that his lips almost touched her ear.

"And you know, I've always been proud of you. You can beat the Freddy slash Freds of the world with one hand tied behind your back. He's got nothing on you."

He pulled away then and guided her to their seats, as if everything was normal. But it wasn't. All that sexual heat had shifted into something completely different. Something that at the moment was scaring the hell out of her. She felt, as she had a lot this week with Max, cherished, and above all, respected. Max didn't toss out compliments about business that often. As they neared their table, she leaned up and said, "Thanks."

He nodded to an acquaintance and kept his gaze directed forward. "It's just the truth. Now, your choice in high-school boyfriends—that we can debate later."

ᘓᘐ

Anna twisted her hands and cursed when the stocking wouldn't give. She'd been trying to ease her hands from the binding since the moment Max started touching her, but to no avail. It should have been easy to slip her hands from the silk stocking Max tied around them and her headboard, but she was finding it unbelievably difficult. Not to mention frustrating.

It was hard to concentrate on the task with her body vibrating with arousal. As Max skimmed his hand up her thigh, her thoughts scattered as her pulse scrambled.

She didn't particularly like this position—under his control. *I need to touch,* she thought as she flexed her hands. She needed to feel his flesh beneath her hands, and *dammit,* she wanted to get what she wanted right *now.* A strange mixture of longing and satisfaction filled the sigh that escaped his lips and warmed her skin. Anna melted a little more. When he reached the top of her stocking, he curled his fingers over then under the lacey edge. He moved his fingers along her skin, smiling when she wiggled in frustration. Bending over, he licked the skin just above the stocking band.

Every nerve ending sizzled, lust spiraled and a wave of liquid heat coiled in her belly.

"*Max.*"

When he looked up at her, she lost her train of thought again. His hair was deliciously rumpled, his eyes hot with intent as the candlelight he'd insisted on flickered over his skin. She couldn't stop the sigh of appreciation. There was nothing so tempting as Max when he was being wicked.

"Anna." He stopped moving his fingers and tsked with mock disapproval. "You get naughty with me, I'll punish you."

"Too late for that," she gritted out but she stilled her actions. She knew Max, and no matter how aroused he was, he was completely in control. He'd lie there all night and wait.

"That's a good girl."

Her eyes narrowed in irritation, but she said nothing else. Because she didn't want the caresses to stop. She'd die if he moved away from her now. Anna was pretty sure she'd combust just from the sexual heat he'd built.

He tugged gently with his fingers, pulling the stocking lower. Slowly, inch by inch, he eased the delicate fabric down. He barely touched her skin. To drive her insane, he followed the same path with his mouth, moving it against her heated flesh. Every few inches, she felt the flick of his tongue, the scrape of his teeth. Anna curled her toes, trying her best not to move her hips. By the time he reached her ankle, Anna quivered with arousal. When he grazed his teeth over her ankle, then flicked his tongue over the same spot, she almost came right there and then. She closed her eyes, willing herself a little more control.

After pulling off the stocking, he slid up her body, his mouth moving over her skin. The heat in her stomach dropped to between her legs, the pressure urging her to press against him to relieve it. He didn't give her the chance. She'd just sighed in relief at the feel of his body weight on top of hers when he pulled away. When she opened her eyes, she found him moving to straddle her by placing a leg alongside each of her hips.

He was still wearing his knit boxers. The bulge of his hardened cock had her licking her lips.

"Ahhh, if you are a good girl, Anna, I might just let you."

Her gaze shot to his, and at that point she almost begged. If it hadn't been for the smug smile curving his lips and the sparkle of devilment in his eyes, she might have. But she resisted the temptation, pressing her lips together in an attempt to keep from pleading.

He chuckled, all too aware of her discomfort. His gaze fastened on her breasts the second before he ran the silk stocking he'd removed over them. "I knew you wouldn't last long. You always have to dive in headfirst."

The challenge in his voice was unmistakable. A lesser woman would have surrendered, but Anna wasn't just any woman. She rose to any challenge, especially from an overbearing alpha male jackass. She gritted her teeth and concentrated on the crack in her ceiling. She would not beg. She mentally read herself the riot act and refused to give in. Her nipples tightened further each time the soft fabric brushed over them. They ached. His ministrations with the stocking were making it worse. There was no relief, but with each pass of the fabric, the tension increased—heightened. She bit her bottom lip to keep from begging for something...anything to relieve the pressure.

The room was silent, save their breathing and the beating of her heart. It was so loud she was convinced people the next county over could hear it. He moved the fabric over her breasts again, wiggling the fabric slightly. She opened her mouth to surrender but he stopped her by bending and flicking his tongue over her nipple. It wasn't what she needed for relief, but it was a damn sight better than the stocking.

Once, twice, his tongue moved over the tip, and then he was gone, dragging the stocking over it again. The silk clung against her damp skin, the friction about killing her. Again, she was opening her mouth to beg, but this time, he swooped in, his tongue stealing inside, giving her a taste of him. Sensual, tempting, delicious. But he moved away too soon for her liking. As he pulled away, she embarrassingly followed him, her lips seeking his for more attention.

"Patience, love."

Desire had deepened his voice, but he still seemed impossibly in control. It was driving her mad to know he was winning, but she wasn't quite sure there was a damn thing she could do about it. And even scarier was the fact she didn't want to. But somehow, he was slipping beneath every defense she had, right into her heart.

But she wasn't given time to think of what was going on in her bed beyond their lovemaking. Max leaned forward and began to nibble on the tender skin just below her jawline. All the panic that had been threatening melted as he moved his mouth over her skin. With tender care, he slowly traveled down her neck then her shoulders. With each touch of his lips...his tongue...her control slipped. There was something different about this, about the way he touched her. It was sensual as always, but it was as if he treasured the act of tasting her skin.

Again, as if he sensed her worry, he moved to her breasts, sliding his tongue over the top of them, then between before capturing a nipple with his mouth. Heat that had been simmering since he stripped her down after returning from their dinner, boiled over. Another gush of hot liquid filled her sex. He said nothing but moved to her other nipple, nipping, licking...

She shifted, trying to ease the pressure building between her legs, causing Max to stop.

"Uh, uh, uh, Anna. No moving around. When you agreed to this, you said you could handle anything."

Immediately, she stilled. He said nothing, but offered her a small smile as he moved down her torso. The scrape of his teeth against the underside of her breast had her sucking in a breath. He nipped at the flesh above her bellybutton. She automatically tightened her ab muscles. When his tongue dipped in, then out, she almost screamed, but she again pressed her lips together.

He slid down her body further, kissing right above her pussy. Anticipation had another rush of wet heat filling her, but he moved to her inner thigh. Settling between her legs, he moved his hands beneath her thighs. With deliberate precision, he kissed and licked his way down her thigh then switched to her other, giving it the same attention.

He held his mouth inches from her sex. The heat of his breath warmed her skin the moment before she felt his tongue slip down her slit, then dip in, barely brushing against her clit. The slight touch sent another tremor through her, almost cracking her resolve not to submit. Curling her fingers into her palms, she drew in a deep breath. He continued the torture. Up, over and in, just enough to drive her crazy. All the while, his fingers caressed her outer thighs. The combination was devastating her senses. The only thought she had was surrender.

"Max."

He looked up at her, his eyes glazed with passion, though there was an air of complete control about him, something she should probably resent, but she didn't. All she cared about was relief. Beyond that, nothing mattered.

Without taking his gaze from hers, he leaned forward, pressed his mouth against her heated core and hummed. The vibration of it wound through her, sending a tremor of heat racing through her veins. She arched her back, ignoring his warning tsk. If she didn't do something, she would combust right there on the bed.

He moved his mouth over her sex, adding a finger, pushing high, deep, as he brushed his tongue over her clit. The pressure built to an almost unbearable level.

When she thought she would explode, when she was a hairsbreadth away from releasing all that delicious tension, he pulled away from her. Frustrated, she growled. His chuckle irritated and aroused her at the same time.

"Give?"

She opened her mouth to offer him a piece of her mind, but the tender look he gave her, the warmth of his eyes and the desire she saw shimmering there had her melting completely.

At that moment, she didn't give a damn about winning, about being the one who could resist. All that was important, all that she cared about was losing herself there, in that warmth.

"Yes."

He offered her a cocky grin then slid a finger into her again, this time pushing his thumb against her clit. She closed her eyes as his mouth covered her again. In the next instant she was dissolving, screaming his name as she came apart. Even before she'd recovered, he was sliding up her body, taking her mouth. She tasted herself as his tongue dove in between her lips. As her body started to relax, he moved away from her.

Max pulled himself up on his knees and said, "Look at me."

It took some effort, but she opened her eyes. The intensity in his gaze almost stole her breath.

"I want to see your eyes when you come." Arousal had deepened his voice, and for the first time she saw the strain to keep himself in check. "I want to see just how you look as you come apart for me again, Anna."

Without breaking eye contact, he took her hips in his hands, entering her with one hard thrust. He groaned her name as he pulled back and pushed in again. The panic that had dissolved earlier came rushing back. He was controlling her with pleasure, and she was allowing it. She'd given him the reins, opened herself to him to control. But in the next instant, he was moving, and damn it all, she lost herself to the feel of him inside her, the passion she saw in his eyes.

With slow, measured thrusts, he built the tension again, pushing her higher, further, never taking his gaze from hers. Fire lit through her, danced along her nerve endings. Soon, his rhythm increased as he pushed deeper each time he entered her. It didn't take long before he sent her hurdling over the edge again, her body shuddering as she moaned his name. But even as she came, he continued his movement, harder, faster causing another orgasm to crash through on the heels of the last one.

This time he joined her, his gaze going blurry with his release, her name on his lips as he leaned forward to kiss her. She was still shivering from her last orgasm as he collapsed on top of her. The only sound in the room was their breathing, and their hearts beating.

Seconds…or maybe minutes later he rose to one elbow, looked down at her and smiled. But it wasn't one of the conqueror, the one who had won the game. It was a smile filled with tenderness. He pushed a few curls out of her face, and then brushed the back of his hand against her cheek. Without a word, he undid the knot in her stockings, releasing her hands.

Pain shot through her arms as she moved. She groaned and winced as she lowered her arms, rolling her shoulders, trying to work out some of the aches. Max pulled her closer, sliding his hands down her back, resting on her rear end. She snuggled close, enjoying the heat of him, the scent of passion still lingering.

"Ah, babe, I'm sorry," he said, rubbing one of her arms. "How about a nice warm bath?"

She licked his nipple. "As long as I don't have to take it alone."

He chuckled. "You got it."

Before she was ready, he was slipping out of bed and heading to the bathroom to start the bath. She settled against the pillows as the sound of water running reached her.

She'd never done anything like that with anyone. She'd given him complete control in bed, over her, over their lovemaking. If she analyzed what that meant, what Max had been trying to accomplish, she'd probably drive herself crazy in the process.

"Stop worrying, Anna."

She found him standing at the bathroom door frowning at her. Ignoring his expression, she allowed her gaze to roam over him. He was still nude, of course, the light of the bathroom spilling around him, and her heart turned over. There was no way she would ever get used to having him look at her like that. She had a feeling she'd lost more than the game tonight, but she didn't want to think about it. She smiled at him, which he returned in kind.

She rose out of bed, ignoring the ache in her arms, and padded across her wooden floor to him. Sliding her arms around him, she said, "Not worrying one bit."

Moments later, she was leaning against him, enjoying the warmth of the bath and decided that for one night, worries about Max could wait. She just wanted to enjoy.

# Chapter Eleven

One of the things Anna loved about owning her restaurant was early mornings. There was something about the bustle of business, the chatty customers and the smell of good beans to get her blood pumping. It is what got her out of bed each morning ready to face the day.

But, in the midmorning lull, she was forced to do the one thing she hated more than going to the dentist. Paperwork and computer work. These days it was worse than putting up with the tedious job. It gave her too much time to think about the one person who inhabited her thoughts more than anything else these days.

She knew she was overreacting, but she still had qualms about the knowing looks they'd gotten from the others at dinner on Saturday night. And if one more person came up to her and said how right they were for each other, she would scream. They weren't. They were polar opposites in all the ways that mattered. Max was a control freak and had been for years. She couldn't deny her enjoyment of the other night in bed. There were two levels to that, though. Max proved Saturday night he could control her in bed, and in her mind that wasn't a good thing. It damn near scared her to death to know exactly what he could do to her. It wasn't just his lovemaking, but her reaction to it. She knew each time they went to bed together, he gained a little more of her soul. Soon, she would do anything to please him, and that was a position she'd promised herself she would never be in again. Max probably knew that and had plans to use it to gain what he wanted. She would not allow that. It was about time he realized it before it went too far. Which, if she were honest, it already had.

Anna sighed in aggravation and scrubbed her hands over her face. Jesus, he was driving her crazy. She was sure Max had some ultimate plan in motion. It would be just like him to plan a freaking courtship because they'd been sleeping together. His outdated sense of duty would require him to do it. Anna knew he hadn't been a virgin before Cynthia, but Anna also knew she was in a different category in his mind than many other women. With their families so close, he would worry how it looked if he fooled around with her, and then didn't maneuver a wedding.

She had to do something to stop the train wreck they were headed for. Hell, he almost married Cynthia out of obligation and they hadn't even had good sex.

Her office phone rang, dragging her out of her morbid thoughts.

"Anna," her mother said.

"Mama. What's up?"

"I talked to Charise and she told me that Max and Cynthia broke off the engagement."

Amazing. Max's parents were still in Greece but his mother made sure to call Louise Dewinter to gossip.

"Yeah, she dumped him."

Her mother chuckled. "Of course. Max wouldn't drop the engagement. It would go against some kind of code. You know how he is."

"Yeah." Sometimes her mother was a bit too perceptive. "Was there anything else?"

"No. I guess Charise is a bit worried that Max will brood over it. Not that she thinks he's brokenhearted or anything. She was convinced that he just saw that Cynthia needed fixing and stepped in."

"Hmmm." Since Anna had thought the same thing she had nothing to say to that. "Well, if you talk to Charise, tell her not to worry. Max and I were out Saturday night and he was just fine."

There was a brief pause, then her mother said, "Oh, good. Because Charise has been trying to get ahold of him and he seems to be out of the office a lot lately. And when she tried to call him Sunday morning, he didn't answer."

For the first time in years, Anna blushed. She remembered exactly what Max had been doing on Sunday morning. It had involved whipped cream and chocolate syrup and licking it off her body. She cleared her throat.

"Was there anything else?"

"No. Charise just wanted me to check. She didn't want to bug you at work so I did it for her. She worries about him and his work schedule."

"Oh, Hank kept the same kind of schedule while he was running the business."

"Yes and he had a heart attack because of it."

That made Anna pause. "Hank had a heart attack?"

"Of course. Anna don't you remember...must have been, oh...it was the year you went to school."

And what a horrid year that had been. "But, you never told me."

"You were so unhappy, and your father and I thought it best not to give you a reason to come home."

She waved that away even though her mother wasn't there. "I will ignore the fact you didn't want your one and only child home with you, but why didn't anyone tell me about it later?"

"I don't know." She heard the shrug in her mother's voice. "I think by the time you returned, so upset things hadn't turned out the way you wanted, we just didn't say anything. Hank cut back, Max took over. Easy as that."

"Max was what, twenty-three?"

"Just turned twenty-four. And you know Max, he insisted. If it wasn't because of such a horrible thing, Max would have thrown a huge party because he'd been chomping at the bit to take over. But, because of that, Charise wasn't really excited over Cynthia."

"I'm getting the feeling that more than one person feels that way."

"Oh, she's nice enough of a girl considering her father, but her whole life would have been wrapped up in being an executive's wife, and Max's need to please, to make sure she was happy would override everything. Charise has always said that Max is too much like his father, including in this."

"Hmm, well, he seems to be taking it okay. He came over that night, we had a mutual breakup party."

And then really hot sex. But her mother didn't need to know that part.

"Mutual breakup? So you and Brent the writer broke up?"

Anna ground her teeth at the question. Instead of correcting her mother on her ex-boyfriend's name, Anna just went on with the conversation.

"Yeah. Anyway, we had margaritas and enchiladas. Max is doing fine."

"Okay. That's good because I really didn't want to come up there. The drive from Pensacola gets longer each time."

Anna breathed a sigh of relief at that. Her parents in town, Max on a mission and the gossip would be too much. It was guaranteed to be an explosive situation.

"Is there anything else, Mama? I've got to get some orders in before the lunch crowd hits."

After she hung up with her mother, Anna's mind started working overtime. All her suspicions had been confirmed by that phone call. Max did have an overblown sense of doing the right thing.

Twenty-four. Although she was older than that now, she couldn't imagine taking over a family business at that age, not one as big as the Chandlers. It was one of the biggest employers in the area so if it failed, so did the economy for their little town. And to have no choice because of his father's health...

She would not be an obligation. Not that in Max's mind that was how he phrased it. He'd been running the show since the start and it was time she took back control. After grabbing her purse, she told Myra she had some errands. The main one being teaching a certain Maxwell Thurston Chandler that he wasn't the only one who had some power.

ꙮ

Max was looking over a proposal for a new ad campaign when Jeanine buzzed in.

She was laughing as she said, "Anna's here to see you, Max."

Delight and warmth spread through him. Anna had been trying to avoid his office since they started sleeping together, worried about the image. Which, again, was odd for her. Anna rarely worried about what people thought of her.

"Send her in."

Anna walked in, offering him a secret smile as she made her way to his desk, and around it to him, resting her rear against the edge. She was dressed in a spandex orange T-shirt that had the name of her restaurant on the front, and another of her full gypsy skirts. He remembered watching her dress that morning, feeling a sense of satisfaction that he'd been there to witness her private female rituals.

"How's work been?"

He took her hand, tangling her fingers with his. "Okay. Just looking over some boring paperwork. How was business this morning?"

"Not too bad, busy as usual." She was still smiling at him, her eyes filled with warm mischief that had his body heating.

She pushed away from the desk and pulled him up out of the chair. Without pausing to say a word, she slid her hand behind his head and dragged him down for a wet, open-mouthed kiss. Her tongue slipped inside, tangled with his. He could taste her, the coffee she'd had and a bit of mint. With that one kiss, his mind was spinning and his cock was twitching. The scent of her drove him insane, coffee beans and wildflowers.

By the time she pulled back, they were both breathing heavily. She smacked her lips and said, "You always taste so good, Maxwell."

"Why thank you." Someone in the outer office laughed, the sound reminding Max that he was at work. With regret, he stepped back. "What do you have planned to do today for lunch?"

She glanced at the door then back at him. One side of her mouth kicked up. "I was planning a little entertainment...something to relax."

It didn't take a genius to figure out her meaning. "Let me finish up here and cancel an appointment I had right after lunch."

He picked up the phone, but before he could dial the number, she sauntered to the door. The click of the lock had him pausing to look at her.

She turned and started back toward him, determined seductress oozing from her.

"I don't want to go anywhere, Max."

Her voice had turned into a purr that had every thought scattering. He was still holding the phone as she approached. Taking the phone from his hand, Anna set it back in its cradle.

"Anna." He tried to sound as if he was reprimanding her, but even he heard the desire threading his voice. It brought about a small smile from her that caused the ball of tension in his belly to tighten. "This isn't something—"

She reached for him then, effectively cutting off any argument. She grabbed his suit jacket, pulled him forward and slid her hand down to his shaft. Cupping him, she kissed his neck. Her breath was hot, the scent of her sweet.

"I don't want to go anywhere. I want to stay here."

She kept stroking him through the fabric of his pants, which sent every available drop of blood to his groin. It had to be the reason his head was spinning the way it was. She grazed the tip of his erection with her index finger. Max had to fight back the caveman in him before he completely lost control.

There was a part of the businessman still clinging to sanity, to keep him from drifting over into idiocy. And that is what this would be. It would be stupid to do something so reckless in the office. It would feel so fucking good, but it was the height of foolishness.

"See, if we left it wouldn't be naughty." Her breath warmed his skin and had his pulse tripling. "And I like feeling naughty, Max." Her voice was only a whisper, but the desire had his blood humming, his balls tightening.

Somewhere in him the sane businessman still lurked because he made one last attempt at stopping.

"Anna, this isn't—"

"What?" She nipped at his Adam's apple and then licked the exact spot. Embarrassingly, he shivered. "It isn't what, Max?"

She moved to his ear, taking the lobe between her teeth.

"It isn't right."

She laughed and another wave of warm breath heated his skin.

"Oh, but how can it not be right"—she sucked on his lobe—"when it feels so good."

As she nuzzled the skin just below his earlobe, the raging caveman took control of his actions. With a growl, he slipped his fingers through her hair and dragged her head back. Bending down, he took her mouth, his tongue immediately invading, as he attempted to dominate the situation. As he pressed his lips against hers, her hand continued to move over his cock. He felt a drop of precum escape, wetting the fabric of his pants.

It seemed for one shining moment, he'd grabbed back command of the situation, of this kiss. He was the one controlling the rhythm of their mouths, and as he cupped her face with one hand, and tilted her head with the other to gain more access, his body and mind rejoiced. He should have known better.

Anna was having none of that and proved it by jerking away from him. Frustration had him scowling down at her, and it mounted when he saw that calculated look in her gaze.

She ran her hands up his chest and pushed at him. It caught him by surprise and, off balance, he fell back into the chair.

Placing a hand beside his head, she leaned forward. The intent was clear in her eyes and he should have known he never stood a chance. Not against her. There wasn't anything he wouldn't do to please her and at that moment, she wanted to please him. Really, how could a man argue with that?

"Listen up, Maxwell." She trailed her hand down his shirtfront to his trousers. Slipping open the button, she said, "This is how it is going to be. I'm going to drive you insane, and you're going to thank me."

With that comment, she slipped her hand inside and wrapped it around his cock. He hissed through his teeth as another pearl of precum escaped to wet the head. She moved her thumb over the tip, smearing the sticky liquid.

As she stroked him, she leaned in for another kiss. Wet, hot and thoroughly erotic. He lost himself in the kiss, in the woman completely seducing him.

Before he was ready, she pulled away. He opened his mouth to protest until she dropped on her knees between his outstretched thighs.

After unzipping his pants, she didn't hesitate. Lowering her head, she took him into her moist, hot mouth.

She worked his cock over, swiping at the tip every time she moved up it. He gripped the arms of the chair trying to keep from losing complete control. And it worked—for a while. Her hair tickled his stomach with each movement. Soon, his blood was draining, his body tightening, his balls drawing up.

It was then that she swirled her tongue around the crown of his cock, and cupped his balls with her other hand. With a gentle squeeze and one more thrust into her mouth, he lost what little semblance of control he had left. With each swipe of her tongue, he inched closer, grew harder.

She added her hand, stroking him each time she moved up his dick. It was that, along with the hum she added that had him coming. In a single blinding instant, he ground his teeth together, biting back the scream threatening to escape and alert everyone to the happenings in his office. It was the last rational act he had before he surged into her mouth one more time. He came, her name a whispered groan from his lips as she continued to suck and caress him.

Mere seconds later, he relaxed back into the chair as Anna slipped up onto his lap and dropped her head on his shoulder. Later, sometime much later, he would worry about decorum in the office. At that moment, he just felt too damn good.

# Chapter Twelve

Three hours later, Max was still trying to figure out what had happened to his self-control. He was sitting in the same position as he had been when Anna had walked in his office with seduction on her mind. Although, he was definitely less tense, he thought with a chuckle.

He turned around and looked out his window, wondering what had prompted the visit. The thought had been nagging him since she did, but he hadn't had much of a chance to get his brain to function after she'd locked the door and used her sweet mouth on him. But now, the worry was starting to set in.

Anna did things like that all the time, but there was something else, something driving her. It was as if...

Well, damn, of course, Saturday night. It had to be that. What scared her about it, he wasn't sure, but it was the only thing he thought might have gotten her to panic. A thread of disappointment wound through him. He was so sure after Saturday night she'd started to accept what was going on between them as something more than just a little fling. All day Sunday, she'd not once made him think she was having second thoughts about their lovemaking that night. But now she was trying to change tactics, pull back. Before he could work through that, his cell phone rang. When he saw Chris Dupree's name, he smiled.

"What the hell do you want?" Max asked with humor.

"Well, since I am staring at your office building, thinking about coming to see you, I thought I should call."

"You're here in Georgia?" He laughed when he realized what he'd asked. "I guess you are if you are sitting outside."

"Had sort of a family emergency that involved Jocelyn—you know my sis moved to Atlanta, right?—so I decided to run on down." Chris sounded worn-out and if he was here in Georgia for his sister, it must have been big since Chris lived in Hawaii. "I thought I should meet up with you, being the best man and all."

Damn, he'd forgotten to call Chris and tell him the wedding was off. Max had been so wrapped up in Anna the last couple of weeks, it slipped his mind.

"What the hell are you doing out there still? Get in here."

Chris laughed and shut off the phone without responding. The two of them were probably as different as two people could be on every level except the business one. Something had clicked when they met in college and the two of them had been the best of friends since.

Max stood and walked to the door. By the time he opened the door, he heard Jeanine's giggle. Chris had one hip resting on the desk, flirting outrageously with his secretary. Jeanine giggled again, sounding more like a teenager than a sixty-something-year-old grandmother.

"I should have known not to leave you alone with her for any time."

Chris shot him a smile, but not before offering Jeanine a wink. "My father always said to treat the secretary like she's royalty."

Jeanine snorted. "I think you need to give my current boss some lessons on that."

"Keep it up, Jeanine, and when Mama gets back, I'll tell her you want to help with the Azalea Festival next year."

"You do and all your files will disappear." With that announcement, she turned back to her computer.

Chris laughed, but even Max could tell there was something missing in it. An uneasy tension had replaced his usual laid-back posture.

"Come on, let's go in here so Jeanine has a harder time eavesdropping."

After settling in behind his desk, Max studied Chris. They were the same age, and both of them had a head for business, an almost sick fascination with it. But that is where the similarities ended. Chris grew up in New Orleans and it definitely affected the way he looked at life. Creole in looks and in temperament, Chris had made an unlikely friend for Max, but then, you couldn't always pick the people you click with. Especially considering Chris' choice in lifestyles.

"So, I hear you aren't really getting married?"

Max laughed at the blunt comment. "Yeah, I sort of forgot to get ahold of you, but since it was about a year off, it just didn't cross my mind." He shoved a hand through his hair. "Sorry about that."

"Hmm." Chris studied him for a moment, then his lips curved. "Son of a bitch. You met a woman."

Damn, there wasn't much he could get by Chris. "Yeah. Well, not met. Known, and now know better."

Chris settled back in his chair as if getting ready for a good show. "So, let me guess. Let me see, someone you know. Have I met her before?"

"No." *Thank God.*

"But someone you knew well enough to fall into bed with..." His eyes lit up and he leaned forward. "What was that kid's name, the one whose family is such good friends with yours?"

Max cleared his throat, damning his friend's intuition. He wasn't quite ready to introduce Chris to Anna. They were too much alike, and damn it all, he had to admit he worried Chris would intrigue her. Good looks, easygoing personality...

"Anna."

"Yes. That's the one, right?"

Max nodded. "Yeah."

Chris hooted with laughter. "I knew you had a thing for her then."

Max frowned at him. "You did not. How the hell would you have known something like that?"

"Well, one, you just admitted it." Chris smiled and leaned back in his chair again. "But you got back to Augusta after a trip down here and insisted on drinking yourself into a stupor, very strange for Maxwell Chandler. Then, while we were out, you proceeded to eloquently tell me how much you wanted to sleep with her."

Stunned, Max stared at him. "I did not."

"Yeah, brother, you did. But I cleaned up your comments. You actually used another word for the action."

Nonplussed, Max felt the heat of embarrassment creep up his face. "Shit. I can't believe I did that."

"I knew you were seriously hung up on the chick when you picked up Diane that night. From what you had said, Anna was the complete opposite in looks. And so were most of the women from then on."

Still stunned, Max shook his head. "Damn. I can't believe you never told me."

"Couldn't. Goes against some kind of male code about drunken declarations or something. Besides, you talked about her more than you talked about Cynthia. That told me all I needed to know."

Max grunted and decided to change the subject. "What's up with Jocelyn?"

All humor fled Chris' face and demeanor when his sister's name was mentioned. "Not really sure. There is just something off and Mama said she needed me to talk to her." He stood and walked to the window. His gaze became unfocused and he said, "Something happened, but she won't let me know what it was. She's lost a lot of weight, and there was something about the way she was so jumpy..."

Max thought of Chris' little sister. Chris had dubbed her the OA, the overachiever. Always first in the class, always determined to come out on top. Last time he saw her she was graduating from culinary school, top of her class of course.

"She wouldn't talk about it?"

Chris shook his head. "I told Mama if Jocelyn wouldn't talk to her about it, she wasn't going to talk to me about it."

"Let me guess, you all argued about it, and she kicked you out."

Chris looked at him and smiled slightly. "No. We did argue but she didn't kick me out. She wasn't talking to me, and she damn sure wasn't cooking for me, which sucked. No one on earth can bake like that girl."

"She's not a girl any longer."

Chris made a face. "Yeah, she said that during one of our arguments. She said she would handle it."

"And she will."

Chris appeared unconvinced. "There is something really wrong."

"There might be. And, knowing you, you're right on the money. But you know Jocelyn. You push, she's going to shut you down. Whatever it is, you have to give her time."

Chris frowned but didn't say anything. There was a tension emanating from him that Max had never seen before.

"Hey, why don't we go out tonight?"

Chris cocked an eyebrow. "Y'all actually have bars here?"

Max tried to look offended. "Yes we do. You know we do."

"One that actually serves, no BYOB."

"You've been here before and we have been out to bars."

"Yeah, but we had to go to Valdosta for that. And sorry, son, I'm not twenty-one anymore. I'm not going to Peaches."

Max snorted at the name of the infamous strip joint just outside of Valdosta. "No, just a regular bar."

"Then you're on. I take it you have room at your place? I mean, Anna isn't going to complain if I am there, is she?"

"No. Besides, I can go to her place."

"Ahh, so you are afraid to let me meet her. I understand your problem. I mean, you are a bit on the boring side, while I have all this hot Creole blood…"

"Fuck off," Max said with little heat. Although the joke did scrape too close to his worries. Not only was Chris a lot like Anna in temperament, but Max had a feeling Chris' tastes in the bedroom would probably appeal to her. Saturday night had proven that.

In fact, they were set to have dinner at her place that night. She had said something about it before she left.

Max pulled out his cell. "Let me—"

"Shit, you're ruined." Chris shook his head in mock disgust.

"What do you mean?"

Chris was already walking to the door when he said over his shoulder, "I'll be out here flirting with Jeanine while you ask for permission for a boys' night out."

Max sighed. He was ruined, and by a woman who probably didn't even realize her own power.

ഇന്ദ

Anna hummed as she walked down the sidewalk to her restaurant. After attacking Max in his office, she'd gone home for a quick shower and a bite to eat. More than an hour after the encounter, she was still happy. Even after Max called her to tell her he was going out with Chris, she held onto her excellent mood.

Hopping over a puddle, she laughed. She hadn't felt this good in a long time. Well, for years. Sex had never been a hang-up with her. There was that one time, but who can claim any sex in high school was any good. Because most of the time you were having it with someone else in high school, who probably didn't know any more than you did.

With all the other men she'd slept with, there wasn't this connection. It should scare her, but she figured her little visit put them on equal footing again. Max needed to know he wasn't driving the vehicle. At least not without some direction.

She was humming her favorite Barry White song when she opened the door. The lunch crowd had dwindled, but a few stragglers remained. It was a good sign for her plans that the college students from Valdosta had started frequenting her place. She smiled at a young couple who looked to be from out of town, but when she turned toward the counter, all the good vibes she'd been feeling dwindled.

There sat Freddy slash Fred, with a smug smile curving his lips. "Anna."

*I should call Max.*

The moment the thought popped into her head, she got irritated. She didn't need him. She could handle this all by herself, although Max would be a sight handier at throwing the dickhead out.

"Freddy. What a surprise." A normal person would catch onto the monotone. Once again, Freddy proved to be abnormal.

He chuckled, in that good-natured way that never failed to make her skin crawl.

"I've been trying to get ahold of you, and when I asked your girl where you were, she couldn't tell me. So, I decided to stay."

Anna glanced at Myra who mouthed *I'm sorry*. Anna nodded to let her know it was okay and faced Freddy. As before, she was amazed he kept his mean nature so well hidden. After what he did to her in high school, it shouldn't. Being older she could appreciate it more.

He stood and moved toward her. Again, she had to remind herself not to back up. She wasn't the little idiot who was positive Freddy was in love with her. He didn't have the ability to hurt her.

Knowing it might turn ugly, she decided it would be best to get out of the spotlight of her customers.

"Why don't we go into my office?"

His smile widened into what she expected Freddy thought was seductive. "Sure thing, Anna."

His easy agreement was tinged with arrogance. As she threaded her way to her office, pushing in chairs and gathering some paper cups along the way, she realized the one great thing about this would be to deflate any thoughts he had of being welcomed back in her bed.

Anna dumped the trash into the can just inside her door and walked to her desk. Irritation had her pulse hopping, not to mention her head throbbing. Once Freddy closed the door, he leaned against it, a smug smile curving his lips as if he expected her to jump into his arms.

"What do you want, Freddy?"

His grin dimmed a little at her tone. "I've been trying to get ahold of you for days. And when I finally did get you alone, Chandler had to bully his way in. You really should tell him you're all grown up now."

"That still doesn't tell me what you want."

"I thought, well, since I returned, I thought we could get together."

Really, he pretended as if nothing bad had happened between them. Had she been so stupid to believe herself in love with him? She must have been. The memory of rushing headlong into a relationship with him still embarrassed her. Two weeks of dating, and she gave herself happily. It wasn't until a few days later she realized he'd used her. And not only for sex, which he could have gotten off just about any girl in school. A bet. That is all she'd been to him.

"I really don't think that's a good idea."

He frowned and shoved his hands into his pockets. "I knew you might be a little sore at me still."

She laughed but there was little humor to it. "Really? And why would that be, Freddy?"

"It might have to do with our breakup."

Was he really that stupid? No, he wasn't, from the look in his eyes. He knew he'd been a bastard, but he was a big enough idiot to think that she would forget what he did to her.

"So, let me get this straight. You want me to date you, despite the fact that you took my virginity on a bet?"

"Ah, come on, Anna. That was how long ago?"

Unbelievable. He actually thought she would let bygones be bygones.

"Not long enough."

"I was stupid."

"Yes."

"I thought by now you would be over that."

He really couldn't be that stupid. But then, he was raised to be a boy king. As quarterback of their football team, along with being from one of the richer families in town, Freddy had been favored in everything. Especially when he hit high school. His good looks, athletic ability and the vintage Camaro his father bought him, made him a leader of the pack in high school. It was the reason she'd been so flattered when he had turned his attention to her. And stupid. She'd been very, very stupid.

"You thought wrong."

Irritation, with a flash of anger moved over his face, but apparently he'd learned how to mask his ugliness over the years. It disappeared as fast as it had appeared.

"Listen, I understand how you might think me a real bastard for what I did." He tried to appease her with a humble smile. Anna figured he must know some really dumbass women. "But, I've grown a lot since then. Matured, if you will."

Not enough to realize that this line wasn't going to work with her.

"I really appreciate that you are back in town, and maybe don't know a lot of single women—"

"I didn't say that."

Ah, well, protect the ego at all cost. "Freddy, I really don't want to pick up where we left off. Because, if I remember correctly, you accused me of being a slut, while at the same time you collected money for getting me to sleep with you."

The silence in the office spoke volumes. He really hadn't thought she would have the nerve to push him on that fact.

"I apologized."

"No, you didn't. But that's okay because I know you wouldn't mean it. It really doesn't matter because I'm involved with someone."

Another beat of silence passed before his lips twisted into a sneer. For a moment, she was eighteen years old, and he had just broken her heart. That same look had been the one he gave her when she told him she was in love with him.

"So, you and Chandler?"

She hesitated and then nodded.

"Mom tried to tell me you were an item. The whole fucking place was abuzz with it the other night."

Oh no, that wasn't good. "Hmm, and you still showed up."

"Well, yeah. I mean, someone like Chandler, he's looking for different material for a serious relationship. Seriously, why would anything develop long-lasting between the two of you? Hell, he was engaged to Cynthia Myers."

Anger sparked through her. It didn't matter if she used the same argument, Freddy didn't have a right to make assumptions.

"And, what, you thought I would go out with you after he dumped me?"

Freddy chuckled. "Of course not. I figured I'd be able to get you to go out now."

"Really? So you think I would cheat on Max?"

"Seriously, Anna." He shook his head and a look of pity filled his gaze. "You *do* have a reputation."

"Well, I guess that tells me. Now let me tell you." For the first time since they entered the office, she let her anger show. She stepped forward and said, "Let me tell you how I feel about you. Even with my tattered reputation I don't want you."

Apparently her true feelings were shining brilliantly because Freddy actually looked...afraid. He tried to take a step back and forgot how close he was to the door. The thump of his head against it made her smile.

"If you were the last willing man in town, I would become a lesbian. You, Freddy, lost any chances with me the day you called me a slut. If you come here to bug me, or my house, or show up at any place I plan on being, I shall tell anyone I know just how"—she allowed her gaze to travel to his groin then back up to his face—"lacking you are in certain departments. You know, so everyone understands the Hummer you have is all about compensating for what you don't have."

His face flushed, either in embarrassment or anger, she didn't know, and really, she didn't care. When he opened his mouth to argue, or call her a slut again, she stopped him with a warning.

"No matter how little you think of me, my family has been friends with the Chandlers for years. One word from me, and you could end up with a few problems with them, and doing business with them might get a tad uncomfortable."

She was lying. Not that Max wouldn't crush him, because he would do it without a thought. But she would never go to him about this.

Freddy didn't say anything before he turned to leave. But, with his hand on the doorknob, he tossed an evil look over his shoulder and a parting shot.

"I heard you became a real ice bitch, so I guess they were right."

She didn't reply as she watched him leave, slamming the door behind him. Alone, she sank into one of the chairs in front of her desk and tried to calm her nerves. But no matter how much she told herself to forget the dicknut and his accusations, her hands wouldn't stop shaking. She figured it was just a delayed reaction, but it didn't stop the sour feeling in her stomach.

Granted, she'd stood up to the bastard finally, but it didn't make her feel any better. There was a hint of truth to Freddy's accusations because she knew her relationship with Max wouldn't last, at least beyond their friendship. The one thing Max cared about was his family business. He'd never give it up and even if he wanted to, no other family members could take his place. Chandler Industries had always been run by a Chandler. Even if a cousin was capable of running it, it really wouldn't matter, anyway. It was what Max had always dreamed of doing. Even in high school he'd talked of it. She didn't fit in with that and she would be damned if she caused him any problems.

Yeah, Freddy had been partially right, but, Anna thought, it didn't mean he still wasn't a dickhead.

# Chapter Thirteen

"Jesus, you *would* pick a place like this, Chandler."

Max glanced at Chris as he sipped a beer and studied the bar and its occupants with irritation. They'd been there for about an hour, and this was the first time Chris had complained, although Max was pretty sure it had been killing him not to.

"You said you wanted a place with local color. I provided." He offered his friend a sarcastic grin and then finished off his own beer.

"I didn't exactly want this much color."

Max looked around Ruby's and realized that Chris probably was right. The décor added a certain backwoods quality to the place. The wooden booths were in sad repair, the bar itself was scratched and worn, and to complete the redneck look, the band played behind chicken wire. Fortunately for them, the band took a break about twenty minutes earlier, and seemed to have lost their way back to the stage. They'd heard enough of the band's singing to know they didn't appreciate the sound of a dying cat.

Chris and Max didn't fit with the rest of Ruby's customers whose average age was probably thirty or forty years older than the two of them. Most younger people headed up to Valdosta for a night out. Ruby's catered to people too damn lazy to drive up the road for a bar with real music and real liquor. The bar had been around for years, probably before Max had been born. The stale beer they were drinking had probably been in the place when it opened.

"Well, this is the only place that stays open past ten."

Chris snorted and raised his hand for another beer. "What the hell did you ever see in this place?"

"I said it was the only place—"

His friend waved away that comment. "No. I mean here, this town. You always seemed convinced that this was the place for you."

When Max turned to face him, his head swam. Maybe five beers and nothing but pretzels wasn't such a good idea. He needed to slow down.

"It's home."

Chris shook his head. "No, it was more than that. It was as if you didn't consider other choices. New Orleans was my home while I was in college, but I knew that didn't mean I *had* to go back home. Thank God, because even though I loved that town, it wasn't where I was meant to be."

Max grabbed the beer just set down in front of him and swallowed the first sip before remembering he needed to slow his pace. "It wasn't as if I didn't have a choice."

Studying him, Chris shook his head again. "You didn't act like it. It was more than that."

Because Chris was jabbing at places Max didn't want to discuss, he tried to change the subject. "Man, you get drunk and get all morose. You used to be a lot of fun, Chris."

"Oh, no you don't, Chandler. I think this is very important. Because, and it just might be the beer, oh and the whiskey chasers, it seems to me that you came back here for one thing."

"I didn't come back here for the business."

"I didn't mean that. I meant Anna."

Max held his head back and tried to focus his attention on Chris but it wasn't easy because the room kept moving. "Give me a break. I came back here after Dad had a heart attack."

"You stayed because of her. I would bet my timeshare on Maui on it."

Max grunted. "Doesn't matter. Can't hold onto her."

Chris laughed and tossed back the rest of his beer. "Why do you want to, Max?"

"Love her." Christ, he sounded pathetic. Pretty soon, he'd end up crying like a little girl. In irritation, he finished off his beer, forgetting again he wasn't going to drink any more.

"Man, you do have it bad. Listen, you're making a mistake with that one."

He closed one eye to focus on Chris. "You don't even know her. What the fuck do you know?"

"I know what you told me in college. Free-spirited and not like you. Your opposite."

Max nodded and almost fell off his stool. After righting himself, he noticed another beer had been set in front of him. Figuring it was already too late, he picked it up and drank.

"So, you think holding on to her is the way to keep her. Tying her down?" Chris asked.

Max snorted then chuckled. "She likes that. She likes that aaaaaa lot."

Chris sighed. "I forgot you become such a jackass when you're drunk."

Ignoring that comment, Max said, "Besides, what the hell do you know about relationships? You are not in a serious one."

"I was. And not a fake engagement like yours."

Max frowned. "I was really engaged. Just didn't really like my fiancée."

"Damn, nothing like the beer to bring out the honesty." His smile faded. "No, I was involved. It just ended."

Max crooked an eyebrow. "Really? I had no idea you were serious with someone."

Which was odd because the two of them did keep up with their happenings. Even though Max didn't understand Chris' choices in life, it wasn't as if he didn't talk to Max about it.

"I was. It was...not pretty. She apparently didn't take me seriously when I said I was a switch."

"So you lost a woman over that. Do you think it's worth it?"

Chris shrugged. "Not so sure now, but she really turned out to be unstable."

"Let me guess, you thought you could fix her."

"No. I didn't. I actually thought she was pretty stable. But that's not going to get me off the subject. Just how long have you had a thing for Anna?"

He was saved from answering that question when the door to Ruby's banged open. Everyone in the place turned to see who entered. Max gritted his teeth when he saw Freddy–the-ex leading the way.

"Well, damn."

Chris turned back around. "Someone you know?"

Max nodded, not taking his gaze from Freddy and his entourage. He recognized most of them. They were the same age as Freddy, all missing necks, all assholes as far as Max could remember.

When he realized Chris was still watching him, Max said, "Freddy Swanson. His family owns a string of gyms in South Georgia. And he's one of Anna's ex-boyfriends."

"Ahh." He turned to watch the group sit at a booth. "That explains why you look like you want to kick his ass."

Max tore his attention from Freddy and looked at Chris. "I do not."

Chris rolled his eyes. "Yeah, you do. You forget you're about six-four and two-twenty. You're not exactly a shrinking Georgia magnolia."

Thinking it best to ignore the jackass, Max turned his back on Freddy and his friends. "I just got the feeling he was still interested in Anna."

"So?" When he didn't answer, Chris answered for him. "You don't trust her."

"No. I do. It's just...Anna has a problem with commitment."

"Ah, so you worry she'll dump you for Freddy."

Max shook his head, ignoring the way it swam when he did. "Nope, just in general. What I don't like is the way she looks when she looks at him."

"Longing? Lust?" Amusement threaded his friend's voice but in Max's mind there wasn't anything funny about it.

"No. It's hard to put a name on it." He picked at the label on the beer bottle. "Something happened there, something she won't talk about."

"In all these years you have been friends, you never asked?"

Max shrugged as he heard a shout from the table where Freddy was sitting. "Nope. Tried to a couple times in the past, she always gets nasty when I do. And not in a good way."

Before Chris could respond to that, Freddy stepped up beside Max, a beer bottle in his hand, and leaned against the counter.

“Hey, Chandler. I don’t think I’ve seen you in here, especially since I returned.”

Max didn’t look at him, just sipped on his beer and looked at Freddy’s companions’ reflections in the cracked mirror over the bar. Their avid interest on the interaction between Freddy and himself was palpable. Deciding it better to avoid any kind of altercation, he took another sip of beer before turning his attention to Freddy.

“And?”

“Just thought it odd. I’m in here a lot of nights, never saw you in here, even when you were younger.”

Freddy’s voice contained a certain high-school-confrontational tone to it. Chris snickered behind Max.

“What do you want, Freddy?”

“Just thought I’d stop by, see what was up with you.” He reached out, picked through the pretzels in the bowl and finding one he liked, popped it in his mouth. He may have been acting nonchalant, but anger vibrated just below the surface. “Why don’t you introduce me to your friend?”

It was as if Max was stuck in some B teen movie complete with bad actors, horrible sets and an overacting bully. Chris wouldn’t quit laughing, which was making it hard to concentrate on Freddy. Besides that, they now had the interest of everyone in the bar. Which meant someone woke up the drunks.

“Sure, why not.” He turned to Chris who looked ready to fall out of his chair and burst into laughter. “Chris, this is Freddy. Freddy, this is Chris.”

Chris cleared his throat. "Nice to meet you, Freddy."

Freddy nodded in his direction. "What brings you to our neck of the woods?"

Chris coughed trying to cover a laugh. "Just thought I'd drop in and see Max."

"Oh, do you work for Chandler?"

Well, of course Freddy would think that. With Chris being black, Freddy wouldn't think they were friends. Chris threw Max a speaking glance. He would only take derogatory comments like that for so long.

"Nope, just visiting the mainland for a bit."

Apparently Freddy didn't know what to say to that because he dismissed Chris and turned his attention back to Max.

"Like I said, with you dating Anna I'm surprised you're here."

Just the sound of her name had every muscle in Max's body going on alert. He'd known from the beginning what this was about, but still, having the dickhead say her name sent a swift kick of anger into his bloodstream.

Chris picked up on it. "Don't let him get to you." He said it so low only Max could hear.

Giving Chris a short nod, Max said, "Freddy, I really don't want to pretend to be friends, so why don't you just tell me what the hell you want and then leave me alone."

The jackass snickered, then sneered at him. "Well, when I saw her earlier she said you two were an item." He shrugged. "If I had a woman like that, I definitely wouldn't be sitting in a bar getting wasted."

At first, a rush of warmth filled Max's chest. The fact that Anna admitted to their relationship was a good sign. Even so, anger slowly replaced it because Max knew the bastard had probably propositioned her. Max clenched his jaw and mentally counted back from ten. Beating the shit out of Freddy wouldn't do any good, and would be bad for business. Leaders of the community didn't get into drunken fights in redneck bars. Although it was very tempting.

He forced his voice to stay calm and took another sip of beer before asking, "And, your point would be?"

Bristling with irritation, Freddy slammed his beer bottle down on the bar. Max watched as the bottle overflowed. Damn, they'd been having such a good time before Freddy showed up.

"My point? If I had a nice piece of ass like that, I'd be home attending to it."

A red haze of fury clouded Max's vision, but apparently the idiot was too stupid to notice how quiet it had gotten and just how angry Max was because he kept going.

"Not like I don't know exactly what you're missing, Chandler. I had a good taste of it in high school, but from what I heard she's learned a bit since then."

When Max looked over at Freddy, he was smiling, not knowing he pretty much had signed his death sentence with that comment.

"Seriously, Freddy, I think you need to rethink your choice in conversation," Chris said.

Freddy laughed as he looked past Max at Chris. "What? Like he's going to defend the little slut? Everyone knows she's just a way for him to blow off a little—"

He ended on a gasp as Max stood, wrapped his fingers around the bastard's neck and lifted him off the ground. His eyes bugged out, and he raised his hands to claw ineffectively at Max's grip. He could squeeze just a little more, snap the bastard's neck.

"Let's be very clear here, Freddy." Max raised him high enough that he had to look up at him and Freddy kicked his legs trying to do anything to save himself. "Anyone says anything about Anna Dewinter, and I'll make sure they regret it. Right now, I'm contemplating on whether or not to kill you."

When Freddy's eyes rolled back in his head, Max tossed him on the floor. Freddy sat up, shook his head a couple of times, but he was fine.

"Well, fuck, Chandler," Chris muttered.

He looked at his friend and noticed the direction of his gaze. He followed to find the no-neck crew Freddy had brought with him had stood and were moving in their direction.

"I should have known when you brought me to this redneck joint we'd end up in a fight."

He stood beside Max, facing the threesome heading their way.

Max sighed as one of the idiots told them that they were about to get their asses kicked.

"And I was trying to act like a leader of the community. This isn't going to look good in the papers."

ꕥ

The ringing of Anna's phone brought her out of a deep sleep. She immediately turned to snuggle closer to Max, thinking to ignore it. When she found the sheets cold, she remembered Max wasn't sleeping beside her. It was odd how easily she'd gotten used to having him there since she rarely liked to have her lovers spend the night.

She rolled over to her nightstand and grabbed the phone. "Hello?"

"Ms. Dewinter?"

"This is she."

"This is Deputy Frank. I apologize for bothering you so late, ma'am."

Turning on the light, she noticed it was just after one a.m. "Was there a problem at the store?"

"No." It sounded like there was a lot of shouting in the background. The sound of scuffling feet followed and the shouting died down to a low rumble. "Sorry about that, Ms. Dewinter, but Mr. Chandler has been a bit loud since we brought him in."

For a second, her mind didn't work. It had to be the sleep or maybe the conversation. "Are you telling me you arrested Max?"

"Yes." She heard some papers shuffling. "Apparently he started a fight at Ruby's, with the help of a Mr. Dupree of Honolulu, Hawaii."

"I did not start that fight, dammit!" Max yelled in the background.

"Shut up and sit down, Mr. Chandler, or I'll have to cuff you again."

Anna had heard enough. "Deputy Frank, I'll be right down."

"Thank you, ma'am. With his parents out of town, I didn't know who to call and his friend, that Mr. Dupree, said to call you."

After hanging up, she rushed around to throw on some clothes. She practically ran down the stairs, almost tripping down the last few. Sitting on the last step, she retrieved her tennis shoes and shoved them on her feet. On her way out the door, she grabbed her purse and keys off the hallway table, then hurried to get to her car. As she sped down her street, her mind raced from one thought to another.

Max had been arrested. Her Max. The guy who rarely went over the speed limit, except while driving her car, and never broke the law. Now, he not only broke the law but got arrested. *For a bar fight.* Jesus, what the hell happened to cause him to get in a fight?

By the time she reached the station, a whole five minutes later, she had worked herself into a proper lather. When she got out of her car, she slammed the door with a little more force than needed. The sound echoed across the almost empty parking lot.

She entered the foyer and even before she opened the second set of doors, she heard Max yelling. And cussing. Never-wear-a-crooked-tie, always-do-the-right-thing Max was using the F-word, and rather loudly.

When Deputy Frank saw her, his relief was palpable. In his late forties, Milo Frank had been a fixture of the police department since he'd graduated from high school. Low-keyed, laid-back and extremely sweet, it took a lot to get the man flustered. Apparently Max had succeeded.

"And another thing, Frank, you are going to regret even thinking of arresting me. Frank? Are you listening to me?"

The deputy shook his head and sighed. "I'm glad to see you, Ms. Dewinter. Although, he got a mite upset when he found out I called you."

Max did not like being ignored. "He's not paying any attention to me, dammit."

"Has he been like that since he arrived?"

"Heck, before that. He cussed a blue streak in the car on the way here."

"Oh, dear."

He nodded. "And if you don't mind me telling you, getting him some help with his anger issues might be a good idea."

She pressed her lips together trying not to laugh. "I'll have a talk with him."

He smiled and grabbed a set of keys. "Chandler's a good kid. Odd I hadn't had a problem with him until now." He motioned with his head. "Why don't you follow me, and I'll release him to your custody."

Nodding, she choked and smothered another laugh that threatened to bubble up. Max was just going to *love* that.

"Man, I kept telling you yelling wouldn't help," another man said. She assumed from the deep thread of New Orleans in his voice it was Chris Dupree.

"Fat lot of good you are. You told him to call Anna."

He sounded like a little boy who wasn't getting his way and it was so un-Max-like that she didn't know what to think. When they rounded the corner that led into the jail area, she swallowed a gasp at the sight of Max.

The first thing she noticed was Max was an absolute mess. His white buttoned-down shirt was torn in a couple places, and smeared with blood. One shirttail hung out and several buttons were missing. Then there was his face. Holy God, what the hell happened? His lip was already swelling, cuts and scrapes covered his face. The hand wrapped around one of the bars was bruised, the knuckles cut and swollen—not to mention covered in blood.

When she met his gaze, she had to press her lips together again. He looked so damn irritated. As if this was all an inconvenient aggravation and no one in the world should arrest him.

"I told him not to call you."

Was he pouting? He sounded like it, although it was hard to tell if he actually was with the swelling on his lip. Anna was sure if she got upset and coddled him, he'd get even more irritated.

Pursing her lips, she cocked her head to one side. "For some reason, I always thought I'd be the one calling you to be bailed out."

# Chapter Fourteen

Max did not look amused by her joke, but someone else in the cell did. His companion laughed, drawing her attention to him. As he stood, she realized he was about the same height as Max, but more lean in build. His skin was the color of mocha. The smile he offered her was mirrored in his warm chocolate eyes. His clothes were in the same disarray as Max's. The blue Hawaiian shirt he wore was about as ruined as Max's. There was swelling above his eye.

"I take it you are the Mr. Dupree from Honolulu, Hawaii?" she asked, returning his smile with one of her own.

"Yes, ma'am. And you must be Ms. Anna Dewinter."

"Enough of the fucking pleasantries." Max gave both of them an irritated look then turned his attention to Deputy Frank. "Can I get out now?"

Frank pressed his lips together as if he was trying very hard not to laugh, but he nodded and stepped forward to unlock the cell door. "Understand, Ms. Dewinter is now responsible for you."

Chris snorted, but neither he nor Max said anything as they walked out of the cell. Max stopped in front of her and stared down at her with a frown.

"I really didn't want him to call you."

If she wasn't mistaken, there was more embarrassment than anger in his tone. For a second, an impossibly long second, her heart stopped and a chill entered her blood. Was he embarrassed by being associated with her? He'd been the one pushing to go out in public more often than she wanted. Anna just stared up into his brooding gaze trying to decipher his comment, but the moment was lost when Chris broke in.

"Ya want to move it along, Max. I've had enough of this jail and I'm looking forward to a bed."

He shoved Max, who threw him a nasty look, but he did move out of the way. When Chris stepped in front of Anna, his eyes were still twinkling with amusement, his lips curved slightly.

"I'm Chris Dupree, since our pal Max seems to have forgotten all his manners tonight." He offered his hand and when she took it, he lifted hers for a kiss.

"Well, it's very nice to meet you, Mr. Dupree."

"That's enough of that." Max snatched her hand away from Chris and practically dragged her out of the hallway into the office. "Let's go."

She frowned but stumbled along behind him. Hearing Chris chuckle, she glanced behind her and saw the other two men following them.

"I'll come by and sign any papers I need to tomorrow," Max said as he reached the door.

"Don't worry about it, Mr. Chandler," Deputy Frank said. "Ruby's isn't going to press charges."

Max came to a dead stop, causing Anna to run into the back of him, then he turned both of them to face the deputy. "You mean I was brought here on false charges?"

Frank rocked back on his heels. “Nope. Swanson was going to press charges. Apparently his father had a talk with him. Decided against it.”

“Fine. Tell Ruby’s to send me the bill for the damage, including that piece of crap mirror.”

With that he dragged her out the door, Chris following close on her heels. Anna didn’t put up any resistance to being treated like a rag doll because that last bit of information had her mind whirling.

Max had beat up Freddy? And just how the hell had that happened? And why?

Max headed for the driver’s door. “Give me the keys, Anna.”

At that she dug in her heels. “No way, mister. You aren’t driving my car.”

He released her hand and frowned down at her. If she hadn’t been irritated with him she was sure she’d find him extremely tempting. Well, hell, okay, she still found him tempting. Especially with his hair all mussed, he just looked…cute.

“You aren’t driving my baby, not as drunk as you are.”

He snorted and crossed his arms. “I’m not drunk.”

She raised one eyebrow.

“I’m not. I was earlier, but I’m not now.”

She settled her fists on her hips. “Really? So, stone-cold sober you use the F-word and threaten Deputy Frank.”

Chris chuckled and she shot him a dirty look. “And you are just as bad. How could you let him do this?”

“Have you tried to stop Max when he’s got it in his mind to do something?”

“Excuse me. I’m still here,” Max said.

She gave him a slight shove. "Kind of hard to miss you. Get in and I'll drive you home."

She unlocked the car, Chris climbed in the backseat but Max stopped beside her.

"I'm sorry, Anna."

She smiled at him and patted his cheek. "You worry too much, Max."

But he didn't return her smile. Instead, he cupped her face in his hands and tugged her closer. It was a simple kiss, just a brush of his mouth over hers. It didn't matter. Her heart still stuttered, her body warmed. Closing her eyes, she lost herself in it, in him. She could smell the beer he'd drank, the lingering scent of his cologne. By the time he pulled away—just a few seconds really—she was breathing heavily.

"I don't want to go home tonight," Max said.

She rested her head against his chest as he wrapped his arms around her waist. Anna was happy to feel his heart beating as fast as hers. "What about Chris?"

"We can drop him off at my place."

Anna pulled back from him. "You'll explain yourself."

He winced, but nodded.

"Okay."

He gave her another hard kiss then shifted away to allow her to slide into the driver's seat. Shutting the door, he walked around the hood of the car.

"Go easy on the old boy tonight. He's a little out of his comfort zone," Chris said from the backseat.

Before she could ask him what he meant, Max was opening the passenger seat door and slipping in beside her.

He glanced behind him. "We're going to drop you off at my house, Chris."

"Tell me something I don't know, brother."

ᘐᘑ

It took close to thirty minutes to get Chris back to Max's house, then drive to her house. With each passing moment, her curiosity grew as did her worry. She knew the only reason Freddy Swanson would confront Max would be over her. And she just didn't get it. He was the one who tossed her aside all those years ago. He could have collected the hundred bucks and she'd have never known.

But she had behaved and waited until Max and she made it home. She turned to confront him, but he was leaning against the door, his eyes closed, posture slumped as if he held the weight of the world on his shoulders. The swelling had gotten worse on his lip, and the cuts and scrapes needed to be attended to. Anna just couldn't bring herself to prod him. He looked completely worn-out.

"Come on, Rocky. Let's get you cleaned up."

Without opening his eyes, he reached out his hand. She took it and tugged him along up the stairs. After helping him out of the tattered shirt, she eased him onto the toilet.

As she opened the medicine cabinet, he asked, "What did he do to you, Anna?"

His quiet question caught her off-guard, although she should have known he would want to know.

Concentrating on wetting the washrag, she said, "He just broke my heart. Or I thought he did at the time." She shrugged and moved in between his legs. Sliding her hand under his chin, she lifted his face so she could see his cuts better. Gently, she dabbed at the one on his lip. He wrapped his fingers around her wrist and she finally met his gaze.

"Tell me."

She'd never told anyone. People at school had known, had viciously ridiculed her. But there had never been a moment she said the words to someone who hadn't heard the rumors. She'd barely been able to admit it to herself.

"We dated for a couple of weeks. He talked me into sleeping with him."

She moved onto a cut above his eyebrow and pretended to concentrate on her task. But, she noticed he winced when she dabbed a little too hard on the wound.

"There's more to it than that."

Sighing, she said, "Do you remember what I was like then? Naïve just doesn't begin to describe me at that age." She laughed wearily. "But, there was old Freddy Swanson, quarterback, homecoming king, and he wanted to go out with *me*."

Looking back, she couldn't even remember the joy, the excitement of being asked out by Freddy. All she could remember was the pain of his betrayal...the embarrassment of what followed.

"We slept together once. Then he dumped me."

She tried to free her hand, but he stopped her by gripping tighter. "Anna." He tugged until she looked at him. "Tell me."

Panic coated her stomach as she blinked to fight back the tears. She didn't want to tell him, didn't want him to know the shame she'd endured.

"I had a certain reputation."

He frowned. "Reputation?"

"I'd pretty much been what you would call a hard sell. Everyone knew I hadn't slept around—little if at all. So, apparently there was some kind of bet. Freddy won."

A few seconds passed before the true meaning of her words hit Max. But when it did, anger returned, stronger than what he'd felt earlier and ten times more deadly.

"I should have broken that son of a bitch's arm." He'd broken his nose, but even that paled to the idea of breaking other various bones in his body. "I should have broken off his arms and shoved them up his nose."

"I think you did enough damage."

"No, I didn't." He looked at the unshed tears in her eyes and silently cursed. Anna wasn't a crier. It took a lot to get her going.

"Max, you're making more out of this than you should."

"Don't you..." *know that I love you.* He shook his head. Of course she didn't. But the truth of the matter was, he had just realized what those three words meant, just how deep the love went. The pain she felt was his. And now he knew why she protected herself. Kept herself cocooned away from commitments. If he prodded, she'd deny it. So there was only one thing he could do. He rose and took her hand.

"Come on."

"Max, you need some antiseptic on those cuts."

He didn't say anything, just tugged her along to her bed. Gently, he took the rag she'd used to clean his cuts and set it on her nightstand.

She opened her mouth again to argue with him, but he stopped her by pressing his fingers against her lips.

"I'm fine, Anna. Truly."

She frowned and he bent his head to kiss it away. Sliding his hands down her sides to her waist, he pulled her closer. In that one kiss, he tried to let her know he was there, that no one would ever treat her like that again.

He stole inside her mouth, tasting her, tempting her. She shivered as he moved away. Without a word, he removed her shirt, then pants, and when she was finally nude, he eased her back onto her bed.

Moments later, when she was still recovering from her orgasm, he slipped inside her, pushing her up and over again, following her as he whispered her name against her skin.

# Chapter Fifteen

Anna gathered her purse and the information that the realtor had given her about several shops in Valdosta. If she wanted to open another location, she needed to plan. And rents in Valdosta were going to run higher than in her neck of the woods.

She hurried out of The Last Drop, trying not to think of the nights she had spent with Max over the last couple of weeks. Each day she felt herself weaken. She didn't like it one bit. If Anna tried to put some space between them, Max made sure he planned something to bring them together. Like her love of watercolors. He found out there was an exhibit of Monet's works in Tallahassee and what did he do? Just showed up and whisked her away on a Saturday morning for a day at the museum and a candlelit dinner.

Max had to know she was trying to keep their relationship a secret, because he tried his best to be seen in public with her. Anna shook her head as she stepped out and shut the door behind her. She spotted Max leaning against the hood of her car. Without saying anything, she continued her task then walked slowly in his direction.

Every hormone in her body bounced to life at the sight of him. Damn, the man was dangerous to her ability to think. A light spring breeze shifted a few strands of his hair. The crooked smile he wore, the look in his eyes—she knew he'd shown up for one thing. And damn if her traitorous body didn't respond.

"What are you doing here?"

He pushed away from the car and his smile widened. "I missed you too, sweetheart."

Even said in a sarcastic tone, the word sweetheart made her heart trip. Men never called her sweetheart. Except her father, and he didn't say it with that husky edge to his voice. *Thank God.*

When she reached him, he leaned down and gave her a swift, hard kiss. As he pulled back, she noticed a couple of old biddies across the street staring at them. Really, she should be mad at him. But with her lips still tingling and her body warm from the brief kiss, she couldn't think of a proper put-down.

"I thought we could drive up to Valdosta, take in a movie, stop for dinner."

"I had plans."

He frowned. She resisted the urge to change her answer just to bring out the smile that did delicious things to her body.

"What kind of plans?" Suspicion colored his voice.

She sighed. "I'm actually heading to Valdosta to look over a few places the realtor sent information on."

"Realtor?"

Was that panic she heard in his voice? No, she had to be mistaken. Max didn't freak out and besides, why would he freak over her looking for a new location?

"Yes. Remember I told you I just started researching the cost of opening another shop? I wanted to do it down there in Remerton, close to the college, but didn't know how expensive it would be."

The tenseness in his shoulders relaxed and his smile returned. “Well, a drive to Valdosta might be just the thing. Plus I could give you my professional opinion.”

She was positive it wasn’t his professional opinion that he wanted to give her. But he was standing there, his hair mussed, smelling of his sandalwood cologne and looking so gorgeous she couldn’t say no. And that made her a little pathetic, but what the hell?

“All right, but you have to behave yourself. This is important.”

He offered her a boyishly sweet smile. “Promise.”

ꟷꟷ

“This place sucks.”

Anna offered the realtor a smile, trying to gloss over Max’s rude comment. “I think Mr. Chandler and I need a moment or two alone.”

The woman flashed them a brittle smile and walked stiffly from the shop. Anna clenched both her hands into fists and counted back from ten. And then did it a second and third time. She didn’t know what had come over him, but for some reason, Max had a bone to pick with every place they’d been. Max had made what should have been a fun adventure into the trip from hell.

“I can’t believe that woman actually thought to offer you this place.”

His tone had become increasingly juvenile and obstinate through the afternoon. At first she’d been shocked because it was so out of character. Max always acted as expected. This was just so...odd. Then, as the afternoon had worn on, she’d moved to wanting to strangle him. Now, she'd just like to stab him with a fork.

She rounded on him, her fists on her hips. "What the hell is wrong with you?"

His eyebrows rose in surprise and he crossed his arms over his chest. "What do you mean?"

The frown he gave her was probably one that would make a lesser woman run screaming from the room. It didn't work on her because she didn't care anymore. He'd pushed her to the limit.

"What do I mean? I mean all the snide comments you made during this trip."

He walked to the other side of the storefront and glanced out the window. The look he gave the grimy glass irritated her. Granted, this wasn't her top choice of places. The space wasn't big enough, the rent was too high and the landlord apparently didn't want to repair any of the damage that had been left by the previous tenant. That still didn't give Max the right to act like a jackass.

"Snide comments?" He ran his fingers against the glass, then made a face when they came away dirty. "I have no idea what you are talking about. All I've done is given you my opinions on a few of the places." But he shifted his feet as if uncomfortable with the subject.

"You call saying this place sucks an opinion?"

"Well..."

"Or maybe the last place? What was it you said...?" She tapped her finger to her chin in mock contemplation. "Oh, yes, you said you wouldn't store the carcasses of dead dogs in it, especially for the price they were asking. You call that an opinion you should share with the world at large?"

"Listen, Anna, I was only trying to help." He shoved his hands in his pockets and she could have sworn he was pouting. And Anna would have laughed if it wasn't hurting so much. Pain coiled in her chest as she looked at him. Never had a man's opinion of her ability to run her business mattered so much. Was everything he said the night at the convention center a lie? She hated to think he said he was proud of her because he was sleeping with her.

She swallowed. "Do you not think much of my business sense?"

His shoulders slumped and a warmth darkened his eyes. "No, I really don't think you need my help. It's just...I don't know. It was stupid, but, well...I just thought I could help you. Be a part of your decision-making process."

The last part was said with such longing it struck a chord within her. "You just wanted to help me. Max, you have a very weird way of showing you want to help."

For a second he said nothing else and the only sound in the store was the air-conditioning kicking on. As if he couldn't stand the space between then, he stepped forward and pulled her against him.

"I'm sorry. I know I was being a pig. I really don't know what came over me."

Anna snuggled closer, resting her nose against his neck. God, he felt so good. The warmth of his body surrounded her. She slipped her arms around his waist.

"Anna?"

His voice had a hint of worry in it so she pulled back just a bit and looked at him.

"It's okay, Max. I just thought you thought I was an idiot."

He cupped her face and bent down to kiss her, but before he reached her lips, he said, "No. I meant what I said. You do know your business. I'm sorry, honey. I'm an ass."

Before she could respond, he touched his lips to hers and she forgot her anger. His kisses were tender but underlined with a hint of passion so intense she felt tears brimming in her eyes. How did this man do this to her? The sweetness of the kiss conveyed deeper feelings. Feelings of want, of need, of more than just a good time.

Anna didn't think, not before this moment, that he would mean those feelings for her. Max was mixing those things up because of their prior friendship. She'd accepted long ago she wasn't the type of woman who inspired that in a man, but as he continued his gentle assault, nipping at her bottom lip, he kept his eyes open. Heat curled in the pit of her stomach. Even though it was not as demanding as most of Max's kisses, Anna knew that this one could be her undoing. Because while her body responded, so did her heart. She wanted to shrink away from the feelings bombarding her. Arousal and fear twisted together, pulling her further under his spell. What she saw in his eyes scared the hell out of her, but what he was doing to her mind and heart was by far worse.

Before she was satisfied, before the fires he had been stoking had the opportunity to flame higher, he shifted back.

"Anna, I—"

The realtor cleared her throat, and whatever he wanted to say was lost.

She looked around Max and met the woman's disapproving stare. "Sorry, but Max is right. This place sucks."

Max chuckled as she grabbed his hand and pulled him behind her. "Don't worry, we'll show ourselves out."

ꕥ

Later that week, Max sat as his desk looking over some reports, and attempted to ignore the worry clawing at his stomach. He gave up the pretense of work and relaxed back into his chair. Running his hand over his abdomen, Max tried to rub away the feeling. But just like the last few days, it didn't work.

He'd like to live in denial, but it was no use. He was too much of a realist. There was something definitely wrong with Anna lately. Oh, she'd been as loving as usual, as playful as he'd come to expect, but...something was missing. She no longer had that little sparkle in her eye she used to have when she teased him.

They'd practically been living at each other's houses for the past few weeks. The nights they'd spent together had come to mean more to him than getting to work on time. And he didn't need anyone to tell him how out of character that was for him. It had never happened before. On top of that, he'd canceled two business trips, and a much-needed board meeting. To others it may seem tame, but to Max, rescheduling trips and meetings was just not done.

He propped his feet on the desk. Max hadn't told Anna he loved her. Not yet. She'd flip out if he told her, and he didn't want anything disturbing her. His plan was working, except for one small thing. Anna was already pulling away from him. Little by little over the past few weeks, she'd erected a wall. Not in the bedroom, never there. Anna gave herself willingly when it came to sex. But the intimacy he wanted—hell, he craved—wasn't there. The knot in his gut tightened. She kept trying to find ways to keep from being seen together in public. Like she didn't want anyone to know they were involved.

Without knocking, Jeanine walked in. "Well, must be nice to be the boss. Taken to long afternoon breaks, have we?"

He dropped his feet on the floor and straightened. "What did you need?"

She eyed him, her soft blue eyes showing her concern. "I need your signature on these forms."

He shook his head to clear it of his morbid thoughts and took the papers to sign.

"You've been a bit preoccupied lately." Her tone was conversational but he could hear the motherly concern beneath it.

"A bit?"

When she didn't say anything, he looked up. She offered him a small smile. "Okay, a lot. And I was glad to see it."

"Sick of having the boss around?"

All humor disappeared from her features. "Seriously, Max, you were working just like your father."

"I thought you liked working for him."

"Yeah, I did. It would have been wonderful to work for him longer, but I didn't get that choice."

He shifted his weight in the chair, uncomfortable with the conversation. Max didn't like remembering that time. Scared out of his mind his father would die. Scared he would send the company down the drain, losing thousands of jobs.

Trying to push away the memories, Max joked, "If you don't like me, I know you have a lot of money in your 401K."

Jeanine gave him a stony stare and settled in one of the seats in front of his desk. "Max, I'm trying to be serious here. Your father almost worked himself into an early grave. You were headed in the same direction."

He frowned. "I wasn't."

"Yes, you were," Jeanine said, shaking her head. He opened his mouth to argue with her but she didn't give him a chance. "Tell me, Max. When was the last time you took a vacation?"

"I went to New York just a couple of months ago."

She sighed. "That was work and you made my point. Until Cynthia broke up with you, you didn't leave in the middle of the day. You never showed up late, that's for sure."

"What difference does that make?"

"Max, your father never showed any stress, just like you. He never had a problem working long hours, he thrived at it. But he almost killed himself. Until a few weeks ago, I was sure you were headed in the same direction."

Before Cynthia dumped him, before Anna.

She rose, her smile returning. "I'll leave it at that, for now. If you even think of going back to the other Max, I'll say something."

He signed the forms and handed them back to her. "You never hesitate."

"I mean it, Maxwell. I really like you better this way. You're happy. Now, I am off to Orlando for the weekend."

He smiled as she walked to the door. "Don't do anything I wouldn't do."

Pausing at the door, she said, "And lately, that means just about anything. See ya Monday, Max."

Once alone, his mind turned back to his problem. Jeanine was right. He was happier...more free. Max didn't ever want to return to the person he was a month ago. Before Anna, before this part of their relationship, she'd always been the bright part of his life. The one person who could always make him laugh no matter what. Losing her, he didn't even want to think about it.

There had to be some way, some plan he could come up with, to get Anna to admit that she loved him.

ꕥ

Anna sat at a table in the back of The Last Drop, filling ketchup bottles. They'd had some heavy traffic the past few days, and she hadn't had time to do the little things that needed to be done. The stress of the job was getting to her. Just today, she'd snapped at Myra for getting someone's order wrong. And that wasn't like Anna at all.

Anna sighed. She knew what the problem was—her relationship with Max. Keeping it at the level it was, not giving herself completely to him, was taking its toll on her nerves. Each day, she woke with the determination to keep herself aloof, to hold back. Max refused to even acknowledge her demeanor. He moved over her like some freaking steamroller. But at night, every fiber of her being wanted to shout out her love for him. His gentle passion, his aggressive play, all of it was driving her over the edge, pushing her past rational thinking.

"Anna, I was wondering if I could take off early."

She glanced up from her task to find Myra eyeing her with trepidation. "No problem, Myra. And I am really sorry for losing my temper with you today."

"Oh, no, I understand." But even as she said it, Anna watched the tension drain from her posture. "With work and your relationship with Mr. Chandler—"

"What do you mean, my relationship with Max?" she asked sharply.

Myra tensed again, and Anna regretted her outburst. The poor girl looked as if she were ready to run.

Myra cleared her throat. "Well, I guess I assumed, like everyone else, that you two were an item."

Oh, Lord. She'd tried her best to keep it under wraps because she was sure she wouldn't be able to handle the pitying looks when Max and she broke up. She could take name-calling and dirty looks but pity…that would be hard to take. Anna looked down, staring blindly at the ketchup bottle in her hand. Everyone in town knew what a catch he was, and if they split, they'd speculate it was something she'd done.

"It's just…"

When Myra didn't finish, Anna looked up. "It's just what?"

"Y'all aren't seen out anywhere really any more than you were before. But he's been here more than usual. And well, Anna, you all park in front of each other's houses. You know how this town is."

She nodded, not sure if she could find her voice. It wasn't that bad. So everyone knew they were having an affair. Big deal. So, there might be a few bumps in the road when they split, but really, why was that so bad? Anna never cared about fitting in with people in her hometown. She loved it here, but that was it. From her teens on, she'd known she wasn't a conformist.

And when they split up, she would move on, push ahead, find someone else. So what if they pitied her? She knew that when it came down to it, both of them would decide that splitting was for the best. She'd been through the pity and embarrassment before—not to mention the nasty whispers. It wasn't anything new.

"It's okay, Myra. I completely understand. Go study for your finals."

Relief filled Myra's face.

Anna stood and started to gather the empty ketchup bottles when the bell on the door jingled. Without taking her attention away from her task, she said, “We’re closed for the day.”

When the person said nothing and didn’t leave, she looked up to find Cynthia shooting daggers at her.

“Oh, I think you may want to have a chat with me. It seems you’ve been fucking my fiancé.”

# Chapter Sixteen

For a moment, Anna couldn't think. Who the hell was Cynthia talking about? Then, like a fifty-pound bag of coffee beans, it hit her. *Max.* She was claiming that he was still her fiancé.

"What do you mean?" Anna asked.

Cynthia walked down the aisle, avoiding the chairs that had been left out by customers. She was dressed in a pale green linen suit, not a hair out of place, her makeup perfectly applied. Damn, Anna hated cheerleaders. And Cynthia had been head cheerleader their senior year in high school.

"I think you know what I mean, Anna."

At first, she couldn't answer because she was a little taken aback by Cynthia's gumption. She'd never really shown any when it came to confrontations. It was one of the reasons Anna had told Max Cynthia was the wrong woman for him. He needed someone to stand up to him. Cynthia would have never said what she wanted with Max, even if she hated every moment of her life.

It was then that she realized Cynthia was waiting for an answer.

Anna shook her head. "No, I really don't."

Cynthia smiled, but with no real humor. "The whole town knows you two have been screwing around for weeks, while I was gone on that trip Max sent me on."

Anna laughed. "Max sent you on a trip after you dumped him? I don't believe that for a minute. Max is a lot of things. But he isn't stupid and he'd never pay for a vacation for you after you broke off the engagement."

Something she couldn't quite define moved over Cynthia's face. Panic? Anna scoffed at the idea. Debutante-trained former cheerleaders never panicked. Not in situations like this.

But, before Anna could figure it out, Cynthia straightened her shoulders and lifted her chin. "Yes, I dumped Max, but we got back together the next day. Didn't he tell you about my visit to the office?"

Anna shook her head, hoping that her shock didn't show on her face. Shock morphed into pain, sharp and to the heart. But again, she hid her reaction. Letting a cheerleader like Cynthia think she had the upper hand could be deadly.

"He showed up late, but you know about that, don't you?" Her smile turned positively evil. "I told him that for the benefit of the families and the business, the marriage should go on. And you know Max—the family business is more important to him than anything else."

Anna swallowed. Her mind raced from one possibility to the next. Why hadn't Max told her that Cynthia came by to talk to him, if he had nothing to hide? No, there was no way Max would use her like that.

"I went on the vacation he'd booked for the two of us, because Max said he couldn't get away." Her gaze traveled down Anna's body and then back up, distaste darkening her blue eyes. "Now I see what was keeping him busy."

A knot formed in Anna's stomach as she tried to ignore the seed of doubt Cynthia had planted. To hide her reaction, she turned and walked to the counter to set the empty bottles down.

Cynthia, apparently sensing her faltering thoughts, went on the attack.

"You didn't think he actually cared for you? Really, Anna." She tsked as if pitying Anna for wearing white after Labor Day. "Max is a businessman. What use would he have for you? He needs someone who could be his partner at home and in public. Could you actually see yourself dressed for a cocktail party, rubbing elbows with some of the biggest names in Atlanta? You know he goes to those kinds of things often, and he needs a wife by his side."

With each comment, she chipped away at Anna's resolve. What had she been thinking? She'd told herself it was another fling, but deep down, she wanted Max to want her forever. But the other night, when he'd gotten arrested, she'd been sure that something else was going on. Max never did things out of character. His behavior after the brawl was enough to make her think that maybe...

The knot in her stomach tightened, and a wave of nausea swept through her. She swallowed her anger and pain, and turned to face Cynthia.

"Do you have anything else you want to say to me, Cynthia? I have work to do." She deliberately kept her voice smooth, hoping to throw her off the hunt.

The other woman's eyes narrowed. "No. I just wanted you to know I talked to Max's parents, and they agree with me. This wedding will happen. Nothing will stand in the way. Especially not some little slut like you."

The pain she'd been hiding swiftly twisted into anger. Anna could take a lot of things, and thought she could handle people saying things about her. Had done so in the past with no problem, but this time was different, especially from the woman Max had wanted to marry at one time.

"Let me tell you something, Cynthia. Whatever you think is going on with Max and me, you are dead wrong," she lashed out. Satisfaction warmed Anna when Cynthia lost her smile and took a step back. Anna used it to her advantage. "And if you ever show your face in here again, you won't leave here looking so pretty. I take offense at people calling me names on my own property."

Without taking her eyes off Anna, Cynthia walked to the door. If Anna hadn't been so angry, she would have laughed when Cynthia bumped into a chair and then the wall. She slipped through the door, leaving Anna alone with her thoughts.

She'd been fooling herself with Max. After all these years, Anna wanted forever. She wanted the white picket fence, but with a man she couldn't have. She didn't fit into Max's lifestyle any more than he fit into hers.

Anger heated her blood. She was mad at Max for letting it go this far and even angrier with herself for falling in love with him. She drew in a deep breath, but it hurt. The anger twisted in her stomach, in her heart. The pain, the regret, the betrayal, sent a wave of icy chills through her body.

Why hadn't he ever told her about Cynthia changing her mind? They usually talked about everything, but he'd never mentioned Cynthia showing up, or that he'd sent her on the trip he'd planned for the two of them. She remembered when he booked the trip as a "pre-engagement" party thing. Max thought it would be good for Cynthia and him to get away.

He'd lied. By omission maybe, but he'd still lied. Oh, Anna was sure Cynthia had dumped him, just like he'd said, but then come to regret her choice. Why hadn't he told her then, before they'd slept together again, before she had a chance to fall in love with him?

She collapsed on one of the stools at the counter, tears now flowing freely. The truth was, she'd always been in love with him. Dammit, she'd walked into this thing with her eyes wide open, knowing that, just like the others, he would leave in the end. So why did her heart feel as if it had been torn to shreds?

Because somewhere deep inside her, she'd hoped Max would be different. He would be the one to stay. But he'd lied. Even as he'd seduced her, he'd lied. And she'd bought it, fool that she was. Anna stood and wiped away the tears. Well, she wouldn't be made a fool of, even by the man she loved. She'd end it her way, the only way, and then somehow pick up the pieces of her life and go on.

ഇ ര

As Max drove to Anna's house later that night, he couldn't fight the feeling that something was really wrong. Anna had said she would meet him at his house for dinner, but when he arrived, she hadn't been around. He called The Last Drop, her house, her cell, and she hadn't answered any of them. Worry knotted his stomach. This just wasn't like Anna at all.

He pulled into her driveway and parked behind her car. Every light in her house blazed, and when he stepped out of his car, the sound of southern rock reached him. A foreboding sense of déjà vu swept through him.

Eager to dispel the worry, he strode up the steps and, without knocking, walked through her front door. She wasn't in her kitchen. Max found her sitting on the couch. The same one they'd made love on the first time, and many times since.

Anna was staring out the back window at the fading sun. She'd tucked her feet up under her, her broomstick skirt spread out around her, a can of soda in her hand.

The blank look on her face had his concern doubling—tripling. It was because of that his voice was a bit sharper than he intended. "I've been trying to reach you, Anna. Why haven't you answered your phone?"

She took a sip of her drink. "You called?" Her voice was distant and cold. His worry increased, and his stomach turned.

"Yes. You were supposed to meet me at my house for dinner. Where the hell have you been?"

She finally looked at him, one eyebrow raised. He couldn't help the anger in his tone and by God he didn't regret it. Desperate panic was racing through him, and it was his only weapon other than begging her. He'd be damned if he'd do that.

"I've been here."

"Cut the bullshit, Anna. What the hell is going on?"

"Nothing. Especially not between us. Not anymore."

She said the words he'd been expecting for days, worried over, plotted to overcome. Even knowing what she'd planned, Max still couldn't fight the shock of the words when she finally said them.

"So that's it? You're just going to dump me like the others?" Something flickered in her eyes, something he just couldn't define.

*Regret? Pain?*

No, Anna had always said there was no regret when she dumped a guy. No pain. It was just over. Nothing left but pleasant memories of a good time.

"I'm sorry, Max, but you know I don't like having a relationship grow stale." She shrugged as if to say what else could she do?

Anger and pain swirled in his chest. "'Grow stale'? Really, is that what you call it, when last night you were moaning my name when you came?"

She opened her mouth to argue, but he held up his hand.

"Never mind. Don't worry about it. Just another of your 'boys', am I? Fine. If that's the way you want it. Just know that in the morning, you have to look at yourself in the mirror. How do you do it, Anna?"

She cocked her head to one side, studying him as if he were an experiment of some sort. "How do I look at myself in the mirror?"

"No. How do you stand being the cold bitch everyone thinks you are?"

She didn't say a word. Her refusal to fight pushed him over the edge. Max leaned down and pulled her up by her arms. Ignoring her gasp, he crushed his mouth against hers in a bruising, almost painful kiss. When she didn't return the kiss, anger had him shoving her away. Her eyes rounded in shock, her face drained of color, but she still didn't say a word.

"I hope that keeps you warm tonight, but I have a feeling a woman like you would be cold no matter what."

Without another word, he turned and strode from the room.

Within minutes, he was speeding through the residential section of his neighborhood, trying to ignore the bone-wrenching pain coursing through him. His fingers tightened on the steering wheel as he thought about her aloof reaction to his anger. Dammit, how could she do something like this to him?

He was different than all the other men before. He loved her. Didn't she understand the difference?

He parked his car in his garage, then walked through the mudroom and into the kitchen. Max stopped cold when he realized all the lights were on even though he'd turned them off earlier. It was then that the smooth sound of soft pop reached him, and he continued to his living room. There on his couch sat Cynthia. A fat, satisfied smile stretched across her face when she saw him.

"It's about time you got home, Max. Where have you been?"

Irritation and anger swirled inside him. He didn't want to deal with this woman when another one was still in his heart, twisting the knife deeper.

"Just what the hell do you think you're doing, Cynthia?"

# Chapter Seventeen

If he hadn't been in so much pain, Max would have laughed at the expression on Cynthia's face. After years of training, of lectures from her mother on how to be the perfect wife for an executive, she apparently lost her ability to mask her feelings. Cynthia looked like she'd sucked a lemon.

"Really, Max, what is wrong with you?"

"Nothing is wrong with me." *Except the woman I love just tore my heart to shreds. Then threw it on the floor and stomped on it.* "What I want to know is what you think you're doing here?"

"Silly." Cynthia sounded as if she was talking to a three-year-old. "I just got back from my trip, and I thought we could have a nice dinner together."

"Why?"

She frowned. "Why?"

"Yes, why would I have dinner with my ex-fiancée?"

Slowly she stood, an indulgent smile curving her lips. "Max, really. I explained that before I left. I made a mistake."

"Cynthia, have you been smoking crack?"

Her eyes widened at his sharp tone. "Max?"

"You dumped me. I accepted. I sent you on a trip we were supposed to take together. Before you left, I distinctly told you that we would not be getting married."

"Well, after talking to Daddy again—"

Damn, he should have called her father when they first split. Cynthia had no backbone when it came to her father and Max knew that. She'd never be able to tell the bastard and make it stick. "Listen, Cynthia, I'm not in the mood to be nice to you. It's over. I don't want to marry you, or your father. Nothing is going to convince me that we should be married."

She sighed, then her shoulders sagged. "It's because of Anna, isn't it?"

Just the sound of her name sent a shard of ice to his stomach.

Before he could answer, she was shaking her head. "Never mind. She denied it when I confronted her earlier today. But the look on your face tells me everything I need to know." Cynthia picked up her purse. "I'm sorry for the bother, really, Max. I just thought it would be easier..."

Anger, swift and deep, had him striding across the living room. He grabbed her by her arms and gave her a little shake. "What the hell do you mean, 'She denied it'?"

Cynthia's eyes widened in alarm, but he didn't give a damn. His life had been torn apart and his pride shredded like yesterday's newspaper. He didn't care if he scared Cynthia. In fact, he hoped he did. He was getting sick of her shit.

She swallowed. "I...I told Anna we were still getting married."

A thousand emotions swirled inside him—anger at Cynthia, anger at Anna for believing her. But, God help him, there was a tiny ray of hope. Hope that maybe not all was lost.

"You told her that this afternoon?"

She nodded and all of it started to fit together. The cold brush-off, the look in her eyes. He released Cynthia as he sorted through everything, trying to define exactly how he felt. Everything was jumbled up and turned upside down. He didn't know what to do next.

Cynthia drew in a deep breath and set her shoulders, as if ready to take on the world. "I'll have to tell Daddy it's really over."

He was damn angry with her right now, but Cynthia, well, she couldn't handle her father, who had an awesome temper and demanded complete control. "Blame it on me."

She shook her head as she walked to the door. "It's about time I stood up to him. I am almost twenty-eight years old. Kind of sad and pathetic that it took this long. Time for me to grow up, I'd say. Tell Anna...well, tell her I'm sorry. Didn't she tell you?"

"No. No she..." Another wave of uncertain, jumbled feelings swept over him. Just when the hell had Anna become such a coward? She was always one to take on anything, head-on.

"I said some nasty things I'm pretty ashamed of."

He focused on Cynthia again.

"What?"

She shook her head. "I'm truly too embarrassed to repeat them. I just...I just didn't know what else to do. The truth is, it was the easy way out. Confronting my father is definitely not something I am good at."

"I told you—"

"No, I meant what I said. I don't want to go through life living it for my father."

He followed Cynthia to the door, his head still whirling, trying to figure out why Anna would dump him without fighting for him. The answer came to him in a blinding flash. Because, every time she broke up with a guy, he claimed he still wanted her. Some would quietly suggest they stay together, others spent money on a multitude of roses, and still others waited around for her to change her mind. She never did.

Again, irritation at her assumptions about him, about the situation, crawled down his spine. She lumped him in with all those damn jackasses she'd dated before. Anna knew him better than that. Didn't she?

Why would she think he would turn away from her to a woman Anna knew he didn't love? Even she told him not to marry Cynthia. He probably scared the hell out of her. Especially after Cynthia opened her big mouth.

Cynthia leaned forward, bringing him out of his musings, and brushed her lips against his cheek. "Thanks for everything, Max." She slipped through the door and closed it behind her.

Max wandered back to the kitchen, thinking about what Cynthia had said. He was shell-shocked by Anna's careless actions and what it could have done to the both of them. If Anna had thought the wedding was still on...

Damn Anna and her preconceived notions on men. Why hadn't she confronted him tonight? She should have ripped him a new asshole if she thought he'd been lying to her. She'd just sat there looking...sad. Oh, God, she had looked so sad. He hadn't realized until this moment what that flash in her eyes had been. It had been bone-deep sadness. His heart ached to think she'd been in so much pain. How could he have missed it?

Max stopped in his tracks and drew in a deep breath. He'd missed it because he'd been so angry at her, at himself for loving a cold woman.

A new kind of anger swept through him. He knew she loved him. It was the only explanation for her behavior. Because she was afraid of losing her heart, she'd almost ruined everything. He drew in a deep breath as he realized that by not telling her how he felt about her, he'd played a part in her misconception. If he had been truthful, instead of planning the whole scenario, she might not have believed Cynthia. Still, she'd allowed him to walk out of her house, out of her life. He grabbed his keys off the counter and hurried out the door to his garage.

If Anna thought she was getting rid of him that easily, she had another think coming.

ജ്ഷ

Anna slipped deeper beneath the bubbles and sighed. Even with Barry White crooning in the background, her favorite bubble bath wasn't making her feel any better. The scent of vanilla and musk, the candlelight, nothing would ebb the pain. She'd drink, but in the mood she was in, she wasn't too sure she wouldn't call Max up, drunk. She would not allow herself that embarrassment. Begging him in the fit of drunkenness would be the last indignity she could stand.

She applied the two slices of cucumbers she'd brought up with her. Her eyes were swollen and gritty. After Max had left, she'd sat on the couch for over an hour and cried. There was no one to call, no one to talk to. Usually when she felt like that, she called Max and they talked, but that was gone now. She would never have him to soothe the pain again.

Anna pulled off the cucumbers and lowered her head as a fresh round of tears spilled from her eyes. Oh, God, it hurt so much. She wanted him here now, to make it go away, to tell her that everything would be all right. She knew it had been for the best. But she knew she'd pushed him too far tonight. Max never lashed out with words like that—not with her. And the cuts he'd left were deep and still bleeding. Well-deserved for what she'd said to him, how she'd acted. She'd done it to protect herself, but she wasn't so sure what she'd accomplished with it.

"Now, why don't you look like a woman who's happy to be rid of me?"

Her head shot up, and she lost her balance and splashed around in the bath water like a fish.

There, leaning against the doorjamb, was Max, his dark-blond hair mussed from the night wind, his chocolate eyes narrowed in suspicion. She reached up to wipe away the tears, but ended up spreading bubbles and water across her face.

"What are you doing here, Max?" Her voice trembled and she cleared her throat, hoping he didn't notice. The sight of him sent a fresh wave of icy pain to her heart.

He ignored her question. His voice was distant, almost cold. "I had a visitor when I got home tonight."

"Oh?"

"Yeah, seems Cynthia told you some lies this afternoon, and you chose to believe them."

"Lies?" Her heart dropped to the pit of her stomach.

"Yeah, you know, where she said we were still engaged. Which I know you understand isn't true. I'd never have gotten involved with you if that were true. What I want to know is why you believed her." The anger and pain in his voice were unmistakable. "Why didn't you trust me enough to ask me about it?"

The stress of the day, the pain from his betrayal, spurred her anger. "Trust you? Okay, why didn't you tell me she showed up at your office the day after you broke up? And that you sent her on the trip the two of you were supposed to take together?"

A flash of guilt darkened his eyes, and she felt the pain of his betrayal as a fresh wound. But he didn't let it last long.

"I'm through answering the questions, Anna. It's your turn in the hot seat. What we're talking about is you trusting me. Besides, if I'd told you, you would have lost your temper."

She stood, her rage dripping off her like her bathwater. "Trust you? Trust you? Dammit, you didn't tell me she wanted you back."

Max pushed away from the doorjamb and walked toward her. The determined look in his eyes sent a wave of heat to her belly. Even as her heart was breaking, she wanted him. She was sick. How could having the man mad at her turn her on?

He grabbed her by the waist and pulled her out of the tub. He placed her on the bath rug, but didn't let go of her. Her breasts brushed against his chest when she drew in a deep breath. The heat of his body warmed her.

"Admit it, Anna."

"What?"

"Admit that you love me."

Panic rose again, threatening to choke her as fresh tears gathered. Did he enjoy causing her pain? Why the hell *did* she love him? Demented. There was no other word that would describe her mental state.

His arm tightened. "I'm not letting you go until you admit it."

Anna swallowed, then practically shouted, "I love you, you jackass."

The next minute, he was dragging her, soaking wet and dripping water on the floor, to her bed. A moment later, he covered her with his body. Her pulse tripped, her blood heated. Not to mention the way her head spun.

She placed a hand on his chest trying to slow him down. “Max—”

“Shut up. Nothing else matters. And I’m going to prove it, one way or another.”

# Chapter Eighteen

The feel of Anna's wet curves pressed against him sent a wave of heat through Max's body. He was still angry with her for not trusting him, but the warmth filling his gut had more to do with her declaration of love. Nothing had ever sounded so wonderful as Anna confirming her love to him, even if she did shout it at him.

He gently brushed her curls out of her face, trailing his fingers along her cheek. Closing his eyes, he took a deep breath. The scent of jasmine filled his senses. Jasmine always reminded him of Anna. When he opened his eyes, he found hers narrowed in anger...maybe. His emotions were a jumble with the roller-coaster ride they'd been through that day. Detecting what she was thinking was hard on a good day. Even if she was angry, he didn't care. She said she loved him. She couldn't take it back. End of story.

Max cupped her face in his hands and pressed his lips to hers. In that kiss, he tried to let the love he felt in his heart, his soul, pour from him to her. Every fiber of his being concentrated on that one thing. She returned his kiss with enthusiasm, even as her tears wet her face and his.

Soon, the kiss turned erotic, her tongue mating with his. Her nipples hardened against his chest, her breathing quickened. As she slipped her hands up over his shoulders, pressing closer, Max knew he had to have her. Nothing else in the world mattered but proving to Anna what they shared was special.

She slid her foot along the back of his, rubbing her sex against his cock. Even through the layers of clothing, he could feel the heat of her arousal. Knowing that he was close to embarrassing himself, he shifted away, standing next to the bed. His hands were shaking so much that he gave up trying to undo the buttons on his dress shirt, opting to yank it over his head. When he tossed it behind him, he noticed she watched his every move. Already aroused, the small smile she offered drove him crazy. Sensuality and love filled her expression. He tore at his trousers, popping the button off in the process. After shucking out of them, he grabbed his wallet and pulled out a condom.

He joined her back on the bed, reveling in her soft, moist skin. The scent of her desire combined with her jasmine bubble bath pushed his own arousal further. Max took one nipple in his mouth while he slid two fingers into her sex. Juice wetted his hand. Oh, Jesus, he had to have her. At that moment, nothing mattered but her. Getting inside her, feeling her tighten around his cock. He drew back, grabbed her by the waist and flipped her over. He shoved a pillow beneath her, propping her ass up further, positioning her just right.

Anna turned around to look at him, her eyes heavy-lidded and darkened with passion. He skimmed the back of his hand down her spine, and satisfaction warmed him as she shuddered. Nothing would ever be as beautiful to him as Anna naked in the moonlight.

His dick twitched with anticipation. He rolled on the condom, and a moment later he was sliding into her as she moaned his name. She was so wet he almost came the first time he drew back and pumped into her. Max gritted his teeth and held himself in check. Still, he had to fight the urge as he continued to slide in and out of her, her muscles clamping tightly around his cock each time. Anna picked up his rhythm, shoving her ass back, taking him deeper. As his blood sped and his balls drew tight, he knew he wouldn't be able to resist much longer.

A second before he lost control, she came, screaming his name, her muscles contracting around him, milking his orgasm from him. He held her still, his fingers digging into her skin as he shuddered, knowing at that moment nothing could compare to that feeling. Seconds later, Max collapsed on top of her, his body slick with her bathwater and sweat. The scent of their lovemaking filled the air as his heart still pounded in sync with hers.

He rolled over onto his back and pulled her across his chest. Her hair spilled over his chest and neck. A little feminine snore sounded, and he chuckled. At that moment, he knew he was the luckiest man in Georgia.

ꙮ

Sunlight streaming through the blinds woke Anna the next morning. At first she tried to ignore it, but the blissful sleep she'd been enjoying was lost to the brightness of the morning. She shifted her weight, trying to get comfortable as she tested her body. New aches from last night's activities left her almost unwilling to move.

Opening her eyes, Anna glanced at the bedside table and noticed that it was past nine in the morning. Late by her standards, not to mention Max's. It was then that it registered she was alone in her bed. She stilled in the act of stretching and listened. There were no sounds coming from the bathroom.

Slowly, she sat up and looked around. Regret filled her as soon as she realized he'd left her. And damn it all, it had been her fault. She'd not trusted him, believed in him. She'd been a coward, and he had left her. Oh, they'd made love all night. Anna was pretty sure she lost more sleep than she got from the night before. But now, in the cold light of day, Max regretted his actions and stole away without saying goodbye.

She swallowed and decided not to cry another tear on a lost cause. It was mostly her fault, she knew that now. And she would be willing to forgive him for not being completely truthful with her. She'd forgive him that because she did love the jackass.

"What's the matter with you?"

His deep voice caught her by surprise. She looked up as Max walked into her bedroom wearing only his dress pants and a wicked smile. The knowing look in his eyes embarrassed and irritated her.

Anna cleared her throat hoping the blush she felt really didn't show. "Oh, nothing."

He handed her a mug of coffee while he frowned down at her. She tried to avoid his gaze as she took a sip of coffee, but she couldn't. He watched her for a few seconds before saying anything.

"You thought I left. Come on, admit it."

"I..." She looked into those deep brown eyes and lost the fight. She was too tired to fight it anymore. Sighing she said, "Yeah, I did."

He settled in a rocking chair she kept in the corner, sipping his coffee for a few moments, then stated, "Stupid."

At first, her face burned hotter. She had been stupid with her assumptions from the first time they'd made love. But, he'd been an equal in this. He'd never told her it was forever, or even tried to.

"Stupid? Are you calling me stupid? Because you weren't here when I woke up and every—"

He was out of the chair in a flash, anger tightening his features. "Don't *ever* compare me to any man you've had in your bed before. I'm not like any of them."

The intensity in his voice, in his eyes, held her momentarily speechless. She gathered the sheets closer, pulling them to her neck. She'd never actually seen him this irritated before. Men hated comparison, but she hadn't made any.

She shook her head. "That wasn't what I was planning on saying." His frown turned meaner and she shrugged. "Besides, what was I to think, Max? We didn't resolve anything last night. We just had sex."

He stared at her, his face now expressionless. His eyes told nothing of his feelings. After a moment or two of his study of her, he relaxed his stance. The smile took her by surprise.

"*Great* sex," he corrected, the amusement evident in his voice.

At first she felt a quick, sharp jab of pain. Aggravation crept down her spine. Damn him for cracking jokes when her heart was breaking.

"And we did resolve one thing. You love me." A satisfied, masculine smile spread across his lips. Irritation was quickly turning into anger. Again, she wondered what kind of an idiot she was for loving him.

She opened her mouth to argue with him, to say that it didn't matter, but she couldn't handle it. She didn't have the energy to fight him, or her feelings. Her shoulders slumped and she sighed.

"Sure, throw that in my face."

His smile widened and she couldn't take it anymore. She had to get out of there or she would disgrace herself by crying and begging for him to stay. That or she might smack him upside the head.

She struggled to get out of bed, but he sat beside her and grabbed her arms. "Anna, I wasn't throwing it in your face. I think it's essential, since we're going to get married next month."

She kept struggling for a second or two after that announcement. She stopped fighting him when what he said finally registered.

"What the hell are you talking about, Max?"

"Our wedding. Do you want something traditional, or do you want to run off to Vegas? We could do it a lot sooner if we do the latter."

The irritation was back, inching up her spine, making her itch from the inside out. "Am I missing something here, Max? I haven't heard a proposal."

"You're not getting one."

She twisted her arms free and jumped out of the bed. "What the hell do you mean? I don't deserve a proposal? You're just telling me we're getting married?"

He looked up at her, his lips set in a frown. "You told me you love me. You can't take it back."

"We already established that fact." She grabbed her robe and shrugged into it. After tying the belt, she crossed her arms beneath her breasts.

"Well, since I love you, we get married. I'm not giving you a chance to think about it and come up with some harebrained reason not to get married."

Her heart smacked against her chest and then flip-flopped a couple times. She looked down at him and saw the raw truth in his eyes. The vulnerability.

Anna reached out to run her fingers through his hair, and wasn't surprised to see her hand shake. Oh, Lord, how could she have missed it?

"You love me?" She ignored the way her voice wavered, and the tears gathering in her eyes.

"Of course I do." He frowned at her, his voice filled with pure male disgust—as if she should have figured it out by herself. "What the hell do you think this all means?"

She shook her head. "Not really sure. You just never said..."

"If I said anything, you would have went running in the other direction."

She laughed, albeit a watery one. "You think you know me so well?"

"I had a plan, and it was a good one."

"And I messed up your plan?" This time she didn't laugh because he looked so serious. "Just what was this plan?"

"I was going to wear you down. It was a sound plan, until Cynthia showed up. Then you go off on a wild hair without even confronting me."

"That was your grand plan? You were going to wait around?"

He frowned at her. "It would have worked."

She laughed as she leaned down and gave him a quick buss on his mouth. Enough for a taste, enough to tempt. When she pulled back, he reached for the sash of her robe. He tugged at it until it came free. She discarded it behind her as Max was reaching for her.

He pulled her closer, wrapping his arms around her waist. "No more calling the shots, Anna." He rested his head against her breasts, and his hands slid to cup her ass. When he spoke next, his breath warmed her skin. "I can't go back to being just friends, Anna. I need you in my life. Lord knows you need someone to keep you on the straight and narrow."

She chuckled, leaning back to look at his face. Warmth filled her, heating her blood, softening her heart. She couldn't think of living without him beside her. Not a day would go by without him there, and she knew that without a doubt now.

Oh, God, she loved him. She'd always known she had, but it wasn't until this moment that she realized how much. Just how complete he made her.

"Anna?"

She wiped away the wetness on her cheeks and smiled. "Okay, you got it."

Relief softened his features, and he smiled that crooked smile that always made her knees weak.

"But, just so you know, you aren't always going to be in charge." She pushed against his shoulder, and he reclined on the bed. Climbing on top of him, she leaned down to kiss him. She could feel his heart beating hard in his chest, his cock hardening against her sex. Anna smiled.

"Now, let's have a discussion about who should be in charge at this very moment."

He laughed then moaned as Anna kissed her way down his chest, nipping at the skin above his bellybutton. It was about time Max learned a thing or two about the pleasures of allowing a woman to take the lead—and she was just the woman to teach him.

# About the Author

Born to an Air Force family at an Army hospital Melissa has always been a little bit screwy. She was further warped by her years of watching *Monty Python* and her strange family. Her love of romance novels developed after accidentally picking up a Linda Howard book. After becoming hooked, she read close to three hundred novels in one year, deciding that romance was her true calling instead of the literary short stories and suspenses she had been writing. After many attempts, she realized that romantic comedy, or at least romance with a comedic edge, was where she was destined to be. Influences in her writing come from Nora Roberts, Jenny Cruise, Susan Andersen, Amanda Quick, Jayne Anne Krentz, Julia Quinn, Christina Dodd and Lori Foster. Since her first release in 2004, Melissa has had close to twenty short stories, novellas and novels released with six different publishers in a variety of genres and time periods. Those releases included, *The Hired Hand*, a 2005 Eppie Finalist for Contemporary Romance and *Tempting Prudence*, a 2005 CAPA finalist for short erotic romance. Her contemporary, *A Little Harmless Sex,* became an international best seller in June of 2005 in its previous novella form.

Since she was a military brat, she vowed never to marry military. Alas, Fate always has her way with mortals. Melissa's husband is an Air Force major, and together they have their own military brats, two girls and an adopted dog daughter, and they live wherever the military sticks them. Which, she is sure, will always involve heat and bugs only seen on the Animal Discovery Channel. In her spare time, she reads, complains about bugs, travels, cooks, reads some more, watches her DVD collections of *Arrested Development* and *Seinfeld*, and tries to convince her family that she truly is a *delicate genius*. She has yet to achieve her last goal.

She has always believed that romance and humor go hand in hand. Love can conquer all and as Mark Twain said, "Against the assault of laughter, nothing can stand." Combining the two, she hopes she gives her readers a thrilling love story, filled with chuckles along the way, and a happily ever after finish.

To learn more about Melissa, please visit http://www.melissaschroeder.net/. Send an email to Melissa at:Melissa@melissaschroeder.net or join her Yahoo! group to join in the fun with other readers as well as Melissa. For chat,

http://groups.yahoo.com/group/melissaschroederchat, and for news

http://groups.yahoo.com/group/melissaschroedernews/.

# Look for these titles

## *Now Available*

Grace Under Pressure
A Little Harmless Sex
The Accidental Countess
A Little Harmless Pleasure

## *Coming Soon:*

Lessons in Seduction
The Seduction of Widow McEwan
A Little Harmless Obsession
Devil's Rise
The Spy Who Loved Her
A Little Harmless Addiction
The Last Detail

*Is it love, or a little harmless pleasure?*

# A Little Harmless Pleasure



Cynthia Myers meets Chris Dupree at her former fiance's wedding. After a little dancing, and champagne, she ends up back in Chris's hotel room. For one night of down and dirty sex. That's it, that's all. He lives far away, and she has other things to do…like get a life.

Chris is a switch. He likes to dominate but he also likes to play the role of a submissive from time to time. His last relationship with a sub turned nasty and since then, he has shied away from anything but straight vanilla sex. When he meets Cynthia, he finds a woman who could change his mind. His mate. The only problem is he has to convince her.

In a carefully orchestrated seduction, Chris teaches Cynthia about submission and dominance, allowing her take the reins. As he leads her through pleasures she thought she'd never experience, Cynthia's self confidence soars and she finds herself falling in love with him. But, when he asks for submission in the bedroom, can she surrender to prove her love or was it all about a little harmless pleasure?

*This book was previously published, but has been substantially revised and expanded for Samhain Publishing.*

*Available now in ebook from Samhain Publishing.*

*Being a spinster was much easier than becoming the accidental countess, and it definitely didn't prepare her for falling in love.*

# The Accidental Countess

*© 2007 Melissa Schroeder*

Colleen MacGregor doesn't like rich men, especially rich *titled* men. Still, her guilt won't allow her to leave Sebastian passed out in the snow. Before he can leave, they are caught in a compromising situation. Under an agreement he will leave and never bother her again, Colleen marries a man she barely knows to save her reputation. Before she can really stop anything, she is whisked to London, where she is transformed into an Original and captures the attention of the ton—not to mention her husband.

Sebastian Ware thinks he'll never see the sharp-tongued spinster again. He never planned on becoming the next Earl of Penwyth...or on falling in love. But before he can declare his feelings, he must protect her from an enemy who wants them both dead. Racing against the clock, Sebastian strives to save them both so he can turn their accidental love into a love for eternity.

*This book was previously published, but has been revised and re-edited for Samhain Publishing.*

*Available now in ebook from Samhain Publishing.*

*Darcy and Mac are "best friends with benefits",*
*but now Mac wants more than just the hot sex.*
*He wants Darcy forever. And he'll risk everything to get her.*

# The Boy Next Door

*© 2007 Jessica Jarman*

The last thing Darcy Phillips wants after the end of a disastrous relationship is to get involved with another man. Being free and unattached was the plan until her old pal Thomas "Mac" MacAllister strolls back into her life.

Mac has always loved Darcy but the timing was always wrong. Now, she's home and unattached. And after a night of wine and conversation, things turn hot fast. But Darcy isn't ready for more than the physical and she definitely doesn't want anyone knowing what the two of them are up to. Especially her mother.

It isn't long, though, before Mac wants more. Much more. Yet Darcy isn't sure she's willing to risk their long-time relationship for something as dangerous as love. But Mac is a man who knows what he wants and he's not afraid to go after it.

Using their incendiary passion as a starting point, Mac sets out to win the girl of his dreams and show her that everything she wants...is right next door.